# GUN LAW AT
# BROKEN SPOKE

# GUN LAW AT BROKEN SPOKE

•

## Terrell L. Bowers

***AVALON BOOKS***
THOMAS BOUREGY AND COMPANY, INC.
401 LAFAYETTE STREET
NEW YORK, NEW YORK 10003

*43376*

© Copyright 1998 by Terrell L. Bowers
Library of Congress Catalog Card Number 97-97119
ISBN 0-8034-9280-4

FIRST PRINTING

PRINTED IN THE UNITED STATES OF AMERICA
ON ACID-FREE PAPER
BY HADDON CRAFTSMEN, BLOOMSBURG, PENNSYLVANIA

For my Uncle Jacob and Aunt Dora,
very special people whom I'm proud to call family.

## Chapter One

Timony Fairbourn was enjoying a morning ride when she spied the marker. At first, she thought the flag was someone's ploy to attract the attention of an antelope. She knew that her brother, Billy, sometimes hunted for game that way, when he was too lazy to go looking for one of the animals. By tying his bandanna on a bush or post, he could sit back and wait for an antelope to get curious enough that he would approach the fluttering piece of cloth to inspect it. There was a saying about curiosity killing a cat, but it was probable that many more antelope than cats had met their end due to curiosity. Following the trail of markers, Timony came upon the two men responsible.

They each had a saddled horse, tied off to a stand of sagebrush, and there was a mule, fully burdened with supplies, including a bundle of stakes. The pair of men both sported week-old beards and each was wearing matching flannel work pants and short-sleeved cotton shirts. Their hats were sombrero types, with a full brim to protect them from the sun. Timony also observed that their boots were made for walking, not for riding a horse. As she approached, they paused from their work to greet her.

"Why, howdy!" one of the two offered, showing a

wide smile that revealed several crooked teeth. ''Imagine that, Digger, a woman, way out here!''

''And as purty as a spring sunrise too, Partee,'' the one called Digger replied. ''Quite a picture.''

Timony did not acknowledge their flattery, but looked at their equipment. ''You're surveyors?''

''Right you are, Missy,'' Partee answered back. ''Got enough to keep us busy for two or three days.''

''You're on Rocking Chair range.''

Partee exchanged looks with Digger. ''I don't think so. We took a read at the Dakota Creek, where the property line starts.''

''Property line for whom?''

''The Black Diamond Corporation.''

''The what?''

''The land controlled by Preston Hytower,'' Digger tried to clear up her confusion. ''He assumed the location of the Renikie ranch some months back.''

''Yes, I know Mr. Hytower and the old Renikie place.''

''Well, this here surveying is for him and his partners. Their claim includes several sections of land, near six square miles. He wants it all marked off, so everything is legal.''

''Six square miles? How can he claim that much acreage?''

''Smart feller, he is,'' Digger spoke again. ''By using the Pre-emption Act of '41, the Homestead Act of '62, the Desert Land Act from '77, and the Timber Culture Act, as revised last year, a man can own up to 1,120 acres.''

''That's still less than two sections.''

''That's where this here cooperative he has formed

comes in. With several others applying for land under the Desert Land Act, they combined it all to form the Black Diamond Corporation.''

''Are you sure this is all legal?''

''I ain't no lawyer, but I'd say so.''

''It doesn't seem possible. The Renikie spread only covered a few square acres, except for the free grazing.''

''Don't know nothing about the local politics of the thing, Missy,'' Partee said. ''We are only driving stakes to show the boundaries.''

''But you're on our land!''

''Map shows only one section for the Rocking Chair. The stakes we planted are right along the west end of your property.''

Rather than argue, she turned to look back in the direction of the creek. ''You marked from the Dakota Creek?''

''Yes, ma'am, both sides.''

A heavy block settled in her stomach. ''Both sides?''

''That's right.''

Without another word, she whirled her horse about and put it into a lope. She had to get home and inform her oldest brother, John. He was the head of the household, the one who was responsible for their ranch. She had to tell him what was going on!

Billy was at the barn, changing out a worn saddle cinch. He looked up, as Timony rode into the yard. He flashed his usual smile, but it vanished, when he saw her worried expression.

''Hey, Sis! Why the long face?''

Timony checked the corral for their older brother's favorite mount. ''John not here?''

"He and Token are out making a count on the new calves. We seem to be short a few head this spring."

She decided to wait at the ranch, rather than go wandering off and possibly not finding him. There was no telling where he and their foreman would be working.

"What's the matter?" he grinned. "You have that sick look about you, as if you've been thinking of your lost love again."

"No! I wasn't thinking of him!"

"Been what, two months since his last letter?"

"Two months, two weeks and three days."

"Thought the guy was in love with you. Sure seems funny, him quitting the letters that way."

"I don't wish to talk about it, Billy."

"Okay, so what's got your feathers ruffled?"

"Have you heard of something called the Black Diamond Corporation?"

"No."

"Preston Hytower has formed a conjoint of some kind under that name. He has placed claim to nearly six square miles of land, including our westernmost pastures."

"How can he do that?"

"According to the two surveyors I came across, he has put claim to land under about every government program ever enacted. Between him and several others, they have 4800 acres."

"Which others?"

"I don't know, but I'll bet it's none of the farmers we settled with last year over the use of barbed wire."

"What are we going to do?"

She paced about, nervously rubbing her hands together. She hadn't felt so in turmoil since her last letter from Luke Mallory. *Lost love!* Billy called him. He was a worthless, deceitful, uncaring lout! *Be patient,* he said. *Work had to come first,* he said, so there would be a future.

*There won't be a future, Mr. Wells Fargo agent!* She fumed silently. *Not if your job always has to come first!*

"You've got a hateful expression on your face, Sis," Billy was keen enough to recognize her thoughts. "I guess I shouldn't have brought up your beau."

"This is serious, Billy!" she snapped. "Preston has those surveyors marking off six square miles! That will give the Black Diamond Corporation control of the entire valley."

"I don't see how they can do that, Sis. We've got our place, there's Fielding and his twelve thousand sheep, plus Big George and Von Gustin. And that's without taking the half dozen farms on this side of the valley into consideration."

"You remember seeing those hard-looking Irishmen in town?" she asked. At his nod, "I'll bet you a dime against your Sunday hat that they have all filed homesteads along with Preston. My guess is, they are all working hand in hand together on this."

"But there isn't any decent farmland left. Without water, those hills won't grow enough to support a half-grown grasshopper."

Timony ceased her pacing and glanced up at the sun. "It'll be dusk in another couple hours. John ought to be home soon for supper."

"He and Token both. You remember that Linda is baking a couple apple pies for tonight. They'll be here on time, you can bet on it."

"I'll see if she needs a hand." She took a step toward the house and stopped. "Will you put up my horse?"

"Sure, Sis," he grinned, "remember the favor when you cut my slice of pie."

Timony displayed a half-hearted smile, but she didn't feel all that cheerful. At the house, Linda, the wife of their foreman, Token, was sitting at the kitchen table, reading a book. Her eyes left the page at Timony's entrance.

"You're home early."

"I needed to speak to John."

"He and Token had a full day planned, but they will be back for dinner—probably in an hour or so."

"Do you need any help?"

Linda smiled. "Nice of you to ask. You've been in a world by yourself the past few weeks."

"I'm afraid I haven't been much help."

"I don't mind, Timony. It makes me feel good to help out."

Timony sagged down in the chair opposite her. "You've been married to Token for a long time, Linda. Does it ever change?"

"What?"

"Having to come second to the job, the bills, the sick horse, the cow stuck in the bog, the weather, everything?"

"I suppose it works both ways."

"When do you put Token second?"

"Our relationship isn't like most others. We don't have children, we don't have a home or ranch of our own. Token worked for and with your father all these years and never wanted more than that. If he had gone out and tried to start his own farm or ranch, we would have suffered the things you mentioned.''

''I don't like it.''

She shrugged. ''It's the man's place to be a provider first and a husband or father second. It's his duty to see that his family has a home, food on the table, a roof over their heads, fuel to heat the stove. It is a big responsibility.''

Timony had never felt close to Linda. She was like an aunt, but she had always been distant and kept to herself. Their woman-to-woman talk was usually a ''hi–how are you?–good-bye'' sort of relationship.

''Is something wrong, Timony? You look worried . . . and tired.''

''I suppose I'm a little of both, Linda.'' She rose up from the chair. ''If you don't need me to help with supper, I think I'll lie down for a few minutes.''

''Go right ahead. I can manage.''

Timony said ''thanks'' and went to her room. Once inside the small cubicle, she lay down on her bed and stared at the ceiling. She had spent many of her free hours daydreaming of the life she had planned with Luke Mallory. For weeks, she had envisioned him riding into the yard, dressed in a fine suit, with a wedding ring in his pocket. Or perhaps the mail would have brought word that he wished for her to come join him at Junction City. It was only a day's ride to the nearest railroad station, then a few hours down the track. She could have left one day and been with him the next.

*But he never came! He never sent for me!* she concluded miserably. *He kissed me, he said he loved me, he promised to come back for me, and yet, here I sit. It's been over ten months!*

It was unfair to not take into account Luke's position. He was trying to run a Wells Fargo office, one that handled the banking, the stage line to outlying areas, the freighting to and from a new coal mine, and a thousand other liabilities. She had no doubt it was a heavy workload, but, if he had only asked, she could have been there to help.

"Maybe he thinks I'm too dumb to handle the books or make change as a teller," she muttered aloud. "I'm a ranch hick with no formal education. What could I possibly know about running a major operation like a Wells Fargo office!"

It had been a long time since she had held her doll, but she removed it from the shelf and cradled it close. How she wished Luke was there to hold her tight. How she missed the strength in his arms, the gentle power of his embrace.

She angrily scolded herself. *Get those romantic notions out of your head, Timony! The man left you behind. Becoming somebody important was always his first priority. Well, he's somebody now—and he doesn't want you around!*

## Chapter Two

The hours seemed longer every day. By the time Luke Mallory managed to close the doors to the Wells Fargo office and grab a bite to eat, he was totally exhausted. There was no rest, not even on Sunday, when he spent most of the day catching up with the book work, checking schedules, and completing other chores that had been set aside during the week. He never had a moment to himself, not even time to write another letter to Timony Fairbourn.

Stretching out on his bunk for the night, he knew that he wasn't being completely honest. There had been a dozen times when he had taken out pen and paper to write. The trouble was, he didn't know what to say. How could he bring a woman into his hectic world? When would they ever have time for each other? He was up before dawn, studied his appointments, outlined the stage and shipping schedules for the day, posted the notices on the company bulletin board, and counted in the day's starting cash for his teller. Then it was an endless host of problems, verifying or handling complaints, doing postal work, running a bank operation, and then witnessing or executing the transfer of everything from titles to land or a house to the sale of a horse or wagon. If he ever finished up, he was expected to dine and entertain

the local or visiting dignitaries. The duties and respon-
sibilities were more than he had ever imagined.

He closed his eyes and tried to form a mental picture
of Timony in his mind. He could see her, the beautiful
girl he loved, with her black, silken mane of hair and
her dazzling blue eyes. He recalled the sweet melody of
her voice. He wanted to be with her, to have her sharing
his life—

"But this isn't what I had in mind," he muttered
aloud.

His appointment as an agent for Wells Fargo had
sounded like a dream come true. It was the culmination
of five years of work and determination. He had attained
an important position in society. He had responsibility.
He was the mayor's right-hand man, the one everyone
looked up to for advice. His life had been a long, rocky
road, from a scrawny, unwanted, street urchin, during his
youth, to becoming the most prominent citizen in the
entire town. It should have been wonderful and fulfilling.
Yet, he was empty inside. A career could not replace the
contentment of a having a wife and family. A man
needed both, but where did he draw the line? When did
his responsibility to his job end, so that he had time and
energy for a family?

A severe knock came at the door. Before he could
even get out of bed, the hammering came a second time.

"Hold back your team," he growled. "I'm coming!"

He crossed the room and yanked open the door. It was
a shock to see Sherman Porter, the district manager,
sometimes referred to as a lieutenant, for Wells Fargo.
The man did not look happy.

"Mr. Porter? Come in. What . . . ?"

"You checked the transfer of funds to our central bank

before you shipped it on Friday?'' No greeting, directly to the point.

"Yes, sir."

"And what was the amount?"

Luke tried to get his brain to function. "I don't recall the exact amount, three thousand and some odd dollars."

Sherman removed a slip from his pocket. "How do you account for this?"

Luke looked at the transfer slip. The amount was less than six hundred dollars. He stared at the signature. It looked much like his own.

"I don't understand. I know the total was over three thousand. We had the monthly deposit from the coal company."

"The receipts that arrived were only pay vouchers and personal promissory notes, no cash whatsoever."

"That isn't possible."

"I need to have a look at your books, Mallory," Sherman declared. "We must clear this up at once."

"I agree," Luke replied. "I'll get my hat and boots."

The two hurried over to the office. Sherman waited impatiently, while Luke unlocked the door and put on a couple lamps. Within minutes, he had all of the receipts and his account ledger open. There was no doubt about the transfer amount.

"Is this your signature?" Sherman asked, pointing to the bottom line on the transfer slip.

"It looks like it. My clerk made out the transfer deposit and I signed it." He felt an ominous dread. "When we're in a hurry, I sign the slip and she counts in the receipts."

"That isn't the correct procedure, Mallory. I must have told you a dozen times, the count must be verified by the station agent before the cash box is locked and transferred to the railroad for shipping.''

''I know.''

''This teller or clerk of yours, Ella Larson?'' he said. ''Do you think she may have altered the amounts?''

Luke felt a rock settle in his stomach. ''There are only the two of us to handle all of the money. I reckon if it isn't my doing, it's got to be her.''

''What of these corrections in the ledger?''

Luke stared at the indicated page. ''Miss Larson has been keeping the running total. I give her the receipts for each day and she enters them in the book.''

''And when did you last check her for accuracy?''

''A week, maybe ten days. We've been about as frantic as a sack full of cats since the coal mine opened up. I turned some of the accounting over to her.''

From the scowl on his face, Luke knew the man was not happy with that answer. ''Summon the town marshal. I think we had best have Miss Larson explain the discrepancies. If my estimates are correct, you are short over four thousand dollars.''

''Four thousand!''

''I'll know the exact amount when I cross-reference your daily receipts with the totals you have been sending us. I'm afraid your clerk has been altering the amounts for some time.''

They made a trip over to the Junction City town marshal's office, which was in the back of his wife's laundry business. Then the three of them visited the rented house at the edge of town where Ella Larson lived, a one-room shack with one curtained window and a dried patch where flowers had once been planted.

The knock went unanswered, so the marshal forced

the door. Miss Larson was not in the house. Her belongings were gone.

"About as I feared," Sherman said. "When I looked at your last transfer for the month, I knew something was dreadfully wrong. The coal mine has not sent any amount less than two thousand dollars since they began shipping their coal on the railroad."

"She sure enough absconded with your money, Mr. Porter," the marshal said. "How do you figure she knew you'd come after her tonight?"

"This was a major theft. I'd say she has probably been taking small amounts all along. When she saw the chance to make off with over two thousand dollars at one time, she couldn't resist."

"I'll have the judge issue a warrant tomorrow."

"Thank you."

Once the marshal had left them, Luke lowered his head in disgust. "I didn't suspect her for a minute. She was eager to help, always asking to take on more of the bookkeeping chores. It never occurred to me that she would steal from us."

"As our agent, you are responsible for everything that happens, Mallory. You should have been double-checking the books, monitoring her every move."

"I know, but there has been so much going on. I didn't have time to handle all of the work coming in. I let her take over that end of the business."

Sherman cleared his throat and stood erect, a man of purpose, his expression stern. Luke took a deep breath and let it out slowly. He knew what was coming.

Billy was restless and it showed. Leta Cline had prepared fried rabbit and made a pudding out of sweetbread and bits of apple. Rather than enjoying the outing, he was troubled by the rumors and latent actions of Preston Hytower.

"I wish you would sit down, William," Leta complained, watching him pace along the shore of the Dakota Creek. "I went to a great deal of effort to show you how good I am around a stove."

"I'm more interested in how *bad* you can be when around me," he quipped, displaying his usual smile.

"You're about as nervous as an expectant father," she ignored his humor. "We don't have much time. Father said to be back before dusk."

Billy returned to the ground quilt and knelt down at her side. "It's this Black Diamond Corporation," he said. "There is a rumor around town that Hytower intends to build a dam."

"A dam, in this part of Wyoming?" She laughed without mirth. "Where would they hold the water, out on the open prairie?"

"The gap at the creek fork might be enough, if they were to build a couple hundred feet of retaining walls."

"Why should they want to dam the creek?"

"So they can have irrigation. It's the only way those Irish farmers can have water for their fields."

She studied on that. "If they took water for their fields, what would happen to those of us downstream?"

"You'd get what was left."

"But we are already using the creek to help us get through the dry months. How can they take that away from us?"

"Preston parades around town like he owns the entire valley. John says the guy has purchased a dozen Hereford bulls and intends to build a massive cattle empire. Those Irish farmers were hired on to claim land and support his cattle with fields of wheat, barley, and corn for winter feed.''

Leta groaned. "I don't like it, William. Just when it looks as if we have a decent life ahead in Broken Spoke, along comes Hytower and his vision of grandeur."

"He won't get away with it. We'll get organized and fight him."

"Pa says he has a ton of money and all kinds of important influence. He's on a first-name basis with the territorial governor, and you've seen his wife! She is escorted around in their fancy barouche carriage, wearing dresses that are the most expensive imported French gowns available. It's easy to see why she married him."

"All I know, is—" Billy stopped in midsentence. Two riders suddenly appeared, riding along the stream bed. "Looks like trouble," Billy whispered, quickly rising to stand.

The two were from the Black Diamond. Billy knew them as Dawg and Chico. They stopped their horses a few feet from the edge of the ground blanket. Billy had heard about Dawg, a muscular man with a pockmarked face and a thick black moustache. He obviously thought a lot of himself, and had already been mixed up in a couple fights since coming to Broken Spoke. Chico was the quiet type, but there was a dark light in his eyes that made him seem the more deadly of the two.

"Wa'al," Dawg drawled, "if it ain't one of our neighbors—no!" He cast a leering eye at Leta. "Make that two neighbors." He uttered a rude chortle. "What do you think of that, Chico? It's a clodbuster and a cowherding man, mixing together like it was almost normal."

" 'Bout as normal as a cat and a dog curling up in the same box, Dawg.''

"You're right, Chico. Turns my stomach. You trying to give a bad name to those of us who run cattle, Fairbourn?''

"Why don't you two keep on moving? We don't want any trouble.''

Dawg, however, was already down from his horse. Chico remained in the saddle, a thin-lipped, sadistic smile playing on his lips.

"You're on Black Diamond range here, Fairbourn.''

Billy bridled. "We laid claim to this land long before you and your greedy bunch arrived in Broken Spoke. Time is a-coming when we're not going to let you push anymore.''

"Tough talk, sonny,'' Dawg said. "Does that mean you're going to push us back?''

"We are going to organize against you land-grabbing snakes, all of us, ranchers, farmers, and even the people in town.''

"Now that frightens me. How about you, Chico?''

"I'm quaking in my boots, Dawg.''

"You got us running scared, sonny. I don't see no way out, but to stand and fight.''

"The fight is coming,'' Billy warned, "if you don't stop pushing.''

Dawg reached out and gave Billy a shove. "You mean like this?''

Billy reacted at once. He threw a right hand that would have loosened every joint in Dawg's body—had he made contact.

But Dawg ducked the wild punch. Then he came back with a couple of his own. He was a conditioned and knowledgeable fighter, Billy was completely over-matched.

Several solid blows sent Billy down onto his knees. Leta screamed at Dawg to stop, but it didn't prevent him from hammering Billy with another punch that knocked him flat on the ground.

Leta charged into Dawg, slapping and clawing, anything to stop him from continuing his pounding of Billy. Chico quickly jumped his horse between her and Dawg, driving Leta backward. It allowed Dawg time to mount up on his horse. Leta ceased her attack and quickly dropped down to tend to the battered and bleeding Billy.

"Let that be a lesson to you both," Dawg sneered. "From now on, no one sets foot on Black Diamond range. You come back, I won't let you off with a warning."

Leta glared up at the two men. "You're a couple big men, aren't you? Big and tough."

"That's right, sod stomper. You think about it before you come onto our land again."

Some very unfeminine words rose to the surface, but the two men laughed and rode away. When Leta turned her attention back to Billy, he was sitting up, spitting a mouthful of blood into the dirt.

"Guess I showed him," Billy mumbled. "Bet his knuckles hurt for a week."

Leta was quick to use a napkin to dab at his split lip, then wet a cloth to put against the swelling around his eye. Convinced that he was not seriously hurt, she attempted to lighten the moment. "As a knight in shining armor, I think you need more armor."

"John never did teach me to fight worth a darn. Wait

until I get home. I'm going to put all the blame on him for getting whupped.''

''Pa told us that Dawg beat up one of Von Gustin's men last week. He loves to fight.''

''Probably a lot more fun when you win.''

''I'd better get you home.''

''Sorry about the picnic. It didn't exactly turn out the way I had in mind.''

''Nor me either.''

Leta packed up the food and blanket, while Billy went to the edge of the creek and washed the blood from his face. A few minutes later, they were atop the wagon, directing the team down the trail. As the dark cloud of the Black Diamond Corporation loomed heavy and foreboding over the land, it was a long, silent ride back to the Cline farm.

## Chapter Three

Luke looked up from the half-empty glass of beer. He recognized Tito Pacheco, his friend and a teamster for Wells Fargo, entering the saloon. He lifted the drink in salute.

"Tito! Come on over and pull up a chair. Give your feet a rest."

The man did so, but there was a scowl on his face. "Mallory, nursing that bottle, you look about as sharp as the north end of a southbound mule. I can't believe you're still drinking away your life."

"What life is that, Tito?" Luke asked sourly. "I don't have a life anymore. Some sneaky, smooth-talking little witch snatched it away from me. She fleeced me like a spring ram, took advantage of me like a green kid."

"No word of where she went?"

"Took passage on a train to Cheyenne, then disappeared. She's probably living like a queen in Saint Louis or somewhere by this time."

"So you're going to sit here and whine, sob in your beer and tell your sad story to anyone who will listen. I always figured you for more grit than that."

"Yeah, that's me, a guy with grit—work and slave for years to get the job I wanted, then lose it in six months, just throw it away."

19

"Feeling sorry for yourself don't look good on you, Mallory. You climbed up from a back-street garbage scavenger to become the most important man in an entire town. That was a real accomplishment."

"And I chucked it out with the garbage, Tito. I plain wasn't able to handle the job."

Tito shook his head. "Are you so sure that you even wanted the job?"

"Course I wanted it! I spent five years hauling freight and working toward that one single goal. When I got it, that's when I messed everything up."

"So tell me, Mallory, what did you like about the job? Did you look forward to going to work each day? Once at home, did you wish for the night to end, so you could get back to the office."

"Well, no . . ."

"Maybe you relished the attention at the different stores or when out and about? I'll bet you enjoyed being on a first-name basis with the mayor and having everyone from miles around showing you all that respect?"

"It wasn't that."

"Then it was the authority, the importance of having your word be law? The handling of other people's money and settling disputes?"

"No!"

"All right. That only leaves the money. You enjoyed the job because of how well it paid."

"Not that either."

Tito laughed. "Mallory, you're a hopeless sot! You just eliminated every reason for wanting to be an agent, yet you're crying in your beer for not still having the job!"

Luke studied him for a long minute. While he had

been in the saloon most of the afternoon, he had done very little drinking. As Tito had pointed out, he was brooding, sulking like a boy who had lost his first fight and had vowed to never stand up for himself again.

"What you say makes sense," he finally admitted. "But why do I feel so lost and miserable?"

"You said it yourself—you worked to become a Wells Fargo agent for the past five years. It was everything you thought you wanted."

"That's right."

"It's plain as the Ace of Spades, Mallory. You don't have a goal any longer. You spent so much time trying to get that stupid job that, now you've lost it, you no longer have any direction in your life."

Luke leaned back in his chair. Was it as simple as that?

"Tell you what," Tito continued, "I've got a load of supplies scheduled for Broken Spoke. How about you ride shotgun for me?"

"Why would you need protection?"

"Okay, for company then. You know what a long, dry haul it is from Rimrock to Broken Spoke. Might even find time to see your gal."

"I couldn't look her in the eye, not after the bust this job turned out to be. I made a big deal out of my new position as an agent. I put it ahead of everything else in my life, even her."

"So you did."

"I wanted to make a success of the job first. I didn't want her to be around if I . . ." he swallowed the humility, "if I failed."

"I'm hauling wire," Tito said, displaying a narrow look, "and something else."

"What?"

"Explosives."

That news caused Luke to forget his self-pity. "Explosives?"

"Rumor has it a couple of engineers have been hired to explore the idea of building a dam above Broken Spoke. I'd say they intend to deepen and maybe widen the gap, where the Dakota Creek comes into the valley. Then a retaining wall would back up water for a reservoir."

"Whose big idea is this?"

"My cousin told me that a new man has moved in and assumed the Renikie place. He used the small ranch to get a foothold. Now he's out to gain control of the whole valley."

"What would give him the right to control the Dakota Creek?"

"I don't know."

"And you said wire? Is the guy going to string wire for his cattle?"

"Again, I don't know."

"You said you talked to your cousin."

"Only briefly. He was in Cheyenne to meet with a wool buyer for Fielding—you remember he owns the sheep ranch in Broken Spoke. Anyway, I guess the old man is ailing. He won't be much help in a fight."

Luke pushed away his glass. The time had come for him to climb up out of his bottle and face the world again. "I'd better settle my bill here. When are you leaving town?"

"First thing in the morning."

"I'll be ready."

\*   \*   \*

On the way to the Hytower home, John Fairbourn rode past the massive foundation for the man's new mansion. It was going to dwarf every building in Broken Spoke or for a hundred miles in any direction. It rankled him that Hytower was the last to arrive in the valley, and yet he intended to run the whole territory. He crossed the yard, the anger building, a single purpose in mind. With a harder than necessary yank, he stopped his mount at the porch of the old Renikie house and jumped down. Tying off his horse with a single toss of the reins, he strode briskly up to the dwelling. Taking a deep breath to control his ire, he hammered on the door with his rock-hard knuckles. Two seconds passed and he raised his hand a second time to bang even louder.

The door opened—

He had been expecting Preston or his foreman, but it was Cassie Hytower who appeared before him. John attempted to mask his rage, but he saw the immediate alarm flash across the lady's face.

"Sorry to bother you, Mrs. Hytower," John said, fighting down his fury. "I'd like to speak to your husband."

She lowered her head submissively, concealing her face with a veil of her auburn hair. "I'm sorry, but he isn't here."

John's anger drained like water through a rusted-out bucket. He was ashamed of the way he had pounded on her door. He had previously seen Cassie from a distance once, at a Sunday meeting, but he had not realized how striking she was up close. Petite, yet wearing a lightweight cotton dress, there was no hiding the fact that she had the feminine build of a mature woman. At his awed moment of silence, she flicked an upward glance at him.

He was devastated by the most dazzling brown eyes he had ever seen. Bright and alert, like two shining buttons, he suddenly suffered a loss of purpose.

"Oh," was the only word he could manage.

"Is there something I can help with?"

He recovered maladroitly, but softened his words, "Actually, I need to talk to your husband about it, Mrs. Hytower."

It could have been his imagination, but he thought the lady visibly flinched at him calling her by her proper name. She recovered quickly. "I have no idea as to when to expect Preston. He doesn't inform me of his schedule. I believe he was meeting with someone today."

John's displeasure was renewed. "Probably with the engineers he sent for. He can't wait to cut off the water to the valley."

"I wouldn't know," she said timidly.

"How about your foreman?"

"Yarrow isn't here either. Most of the time Preston's uncle, Mont Hytower, stays close by. Other than for him, I'm usually pretty much alone during the day."

John looked at the solitary bunkhouse. "No other women on the place?"

"None of the men working for Preston are married, although a couple have female companions over on occasion."

"You speak like an educated woman."

"Not formally, but Preston hired a tutor for me, so I would be presentable. It's important that I don't embarrass him at social gatherings or when we're around important people."

He didn't know exactly why, but her explanation left a sour taste in his mouth. John took a moment to study the lady, but she refused eye contact. She was shy, not coy, he deduced. Preston wanted her to talk like an educated woman, to be a proper lady. That made sense, as the man probably knew senators, statesmen, and governors by their first names. Cassie's grammar was near perfect, but she definitely lacked the confidence to look another person squarely in the eye.

"I've never spoken to your husband. Did I hear correctly, that you moved here from Philadelphia?"

"Yes."

"How did you meet him, at a big charity ball or something?"

"No."

"I suppose that's personal. I apologize for prying."

Cassie stared at her feet for a few long seconds. John backed up a step, about to say good-bye, when she suddenly said: "If you want to wait around a few minutes, I have some rather tangy applejack or I can offer you a cup of coffee."

"I wouldn't want to be a bother."

The lady hesitated, then took a swift look around the yard. There was no one in sight. This time, when she raised her eyes, she held his own with a magnetism that had his boots nailed to the porch.

"It's no bother, Mr. Fairbourn. As I said, there are no other women on the ranch, and we're not exactly popular in the valley. I actually get quite lonely at times."

"I'm surprised Preston doesn't have himself a few servants."

"Only Uncle Mont for the time being. He is too along in years to do any strenuous work, but he is pleasant company and something of a handyman."

"I hadn't heard anything about a second Hytower living here."

"Mont worked with Preston's father for twenty-five years. When Garth Hytower died last year, Preston invited Mont to join us in the move to Wyoming territory. He acts as my escort or driver, whenever Preston is not available."

"I see."

"And of course, Preston has promised to hire servants, once we get the new house built. At the moment, I do all the cooking for the men."

"Must be quite a chore," he said, wondering how many men she was referring to.

"Often, it's only Mont, Preston, and usually Yarrow," she oddly answered his question. "Sometimes, there is also Mr. Dawg or the two hired hands, Chico and Quanto. The Irish don't eat with us."

"I imagine they are busy improving on their homesteads."

"I suppose."

"Did you know your husband and the Irish farmers have staked land that belonged to some of us ranchers?"

Cassie sighed. "I'm not informed about what Preston is doing, but I am not blind to the anger and contempt from the people in town. It's very difficult to not have any friends."

John was moved by the sadness in her voice. "Maybe you could visit us sometime. My sister tires of having mostly men on our ranch all the time. Other than my foreman's wife, she is pretty much alone too."

"That would be nice, but I couldn't."

"Why not?"

"I'm sure Preston wouldn't allow it."

Before John could say another word, a rider came into the yard. He saw an instant alarm spring into the girl's face. She even took an involuntary step backward.

"You have to go!" she whispered frantically. "Hurry! I can't talk to you!"

The man pulled his horse to a stop a few feet from the house. John had not spoken to him but he knew a little about the man called Yarrow. He was Preston's foreman, built lean and deadly, about as endearing as a rattlesnake with arms and legs. From atop his horse, he surveyed the two of them with an apathetic gaze.

John observed the hawkish face, which sported a hook nose and suspicious eyes, deep-set under bushy brows. A sneer of contempt curled the man's thin lips.

"You shouldn't be entertaining gentlemen at the house when Preston ain't home, Mrs. Hytower. Might give people the wrong idea."

John shot a glance at Cassie and saw the color drain from her face. It struck a sensitive nerve that she was immediately cowed.

"Mr. Fairbourn was only asking when Preston would be home," she replied in a fearful and shrinking voice. "I didn't do anything wrong."

"I'm sure you didn't," Yarrow replied callously. He swung a leg over the back of his horse and stepped down. "But you know how narrow-minded Preston can be. He might not think along the same lines."

John didn't like Yarrow's condescending manner toward the young woman. With a deliberate move, he took a step and planted himself in front of Yarrow. He stood an inch or two taller than the man, with an easy twenty pounds of weight difference. With a deliberate insolence, he glared down at Yarrow.

"You've got a real careless way of speaking to a lady, mister. Mrs. Hytower was only being hospitable. If you think otherwise, maybe you'd like to step out into the yard and I'll explain it to you in terms you can understand."

Yarrow did not back water, but neither did he accept the challenge. Instead, he grinned without mirth. "I suppose you're used to casting the big shadow around Broken Spoke, Fairbourn, but it ain't going to be that way much longer."

"Exactly my reason for being here, Yarrow. What kind of underhanded deal is your boss trying to pull?"

"Ain't nothing underhanded about it, Fairbourn. Mr. Hytower is taking advantage of the laws of the land, that's all."

"By claiming property that isn't rightly his?"

"Check the deeds at the recorder's office in Cheyenne. We ain't staked nothing but unclaimed land for improvement."

"Dawg attacked my little brother for no reason too."

"Not the way I heard it. Story was your brother was on our property and got smart with him. I'd say he asked for a black eye."

"When is your boss due back?"

"Not till late—maybe not tonight at all. He doesn't clear his schedule with me."

"You tell the big bull I want a word with him," John told him. Then, with another hard stare, "and if you have anything else to say about my speaking to the lady here, we can still settle that between us."

Yarrow's face worked, the muscles tightening about his jaw. However, he displayed another smirk.

"Maybe some other time, Fairbourn. I don't dirty my hands unless I have the say-so from the boss."

John took a moment to rotate about and tip his hat to Cassie. "Pleasure to have met you, Mrs. Hytower. Good day to you."

She did not reply, but gave a minute nod of her head in response.

John purposely brushed by Yarrow, forcing him to step aside. He mounted up and, without a backward glance, neck-reined his horse around and put the gelding into a lope. The trip had settled nothing, but he was convinced his fears were not unfounded. Hytower had put claim to a lot of land, land he had to develop. That meant getting water to the farmland his Irish counterparts had claimed. The Dakota Creek did not run enough water to provide irrigation for any new farms. He recalled that Timony had said something about the Timber-Culture Act. Cartwell Devine, the town mayor, had told him about a change in that law, reducing the number of acres that had to be put into trees. Ten acres came to mind.

*Even so, no one could plant ten acres of trees and expect them to grow without water!*

John slowed his horse to a walk, turning over ideas in his head. He had some trouble maintaining the focus of his thoughts. Cassie's reaction to Yarrow's threat stood out in his mind. She was frightened of something—no, terrified was more like it. Whether it was fear of Preston or Yarrow himself, he didn't know. However, it went against the grain to see anyone with that kind of fear of another person. He had known a man or two who felt justified to treat a woman like property, including occasionally dishing out some abuse. He had been raised by a man who revered his wife, and she, in turn, was utterly devoted to him. It was the way a man and wife should behave. The ugliness of fighting was too abhorrent to even dwell upon. Especially, if the arguments turned physical. There was seldom an excuse for a man to hit a woman—none, in fact, that he could think of at the moment.

He gnashed his teeth and gripped the reins tightly. The idea that Preston might mistreat his lovely young wife tied a knot in his stomach and filled him with a burning rage. He attempted to tell himself it was not his concern, none of his business, but it still haunted him unmercifully.

''If I thought that miserable swine ever hit her,'' he vowed aloud, ''I'd stomp the slimy vermin into a puddle!''

It was an empty threat, for he was unlikely to learn when and if Preston ever took out his anger on Cassie.

There was a second possibility to consider. Her fear could have been of Yarrow. It was unlikely, but the man obviously delighted in toying with and taunting the woman. It might be harmless teasing, but John couldn't be certain of that. He settled into the saddle for the ride home, disappointed in having wasted a trip. He'd gotten no satisfaction about the attack on Billy and no answers to his questions about the dam or the new boundaries. The vehemence and fury he felt remained.

He tried to redirect his thoughts to the problems and trouble looming for all the farmers and ranchers in Broken Spoke. He could ill afford to be pining over the fate of someone's wife. Cassie had promised Preston her love and fidelity. There was nothing about her life that was his business!

The notion echoed in his head, but there was no conviction. Something about the girl stirred him deeply. He was stricken by her guileless brown eyes, the meekness of her manner, her pure innocence. No matter what he told himself, he couldn't rid the image from his mind.

"Dad blame it, John!" he cussed his brooding, "get your head on straight. The gal is married!"

## Chapter Four

The memories all flooded back, as Luke entered town at Tito's side. The wagon rolled until Tito drew up the team in front of the livery. A bearded man, built like a scarecrow, wandered out of the shade. Luke saw Bunion's eyes grow wide with surprise.

"Well, bless my corns! Howdy do, Mallory! Tito!" He showed a toothy smile. "Fancy the two of you returning to Broken Spoke."

"How's the livery business, Bunion?"

"Going great. There's a new stallion prancing the hills. He has been sending a lot of work my way."

"Name of Hytower?" Tito asked.

"That's the feller."

"We've brought him a load of freight."

Bunion gave a narrow wink. "Frieght, that's what you call a ton of dynamite?"

"You know about the explosives?"

"Not much escapes me, Tito. You remember that Cole is my pard, and he is still the telegrapher. I knew about the order a week before you got it."

Luke looked up the street. The town hadn't changed. He could see the tiny office that served for the jail and telegraph office. The Ace High Saloon still needed a new coat of stain for the false front. It was familiar, yet somehow different. When he had last been to Broken Spoke, he had been a teamster hauling barbed wire. It had caused a fight, he was nearly hanged, and had ended up wearing a deputy's badge. Along with the excitement, he had found and fallen in love with a beautiful woman. On that last count, he didn't know what kind of reception she would give him, but he had to get up the nerve up to find out.

"This new man in town, Hytower?" Luke asked. "What's the story on him?"

"He wants to run a Hereford mix of cattle and set himself up with the biggest ranch in Wyoming territory."

"Ambitious."

"More than that, he's got a ton of money." Bunion uttered a grunt of contempt. "His old man got rich on a mill shop back east; I hear from working kids and women for twelve hours a day and paying them pennies. Now the old boy has died and his boy wants to do something different, be the big bear of the woods, and he's done chosen Broken Spoke as his forest."

"Money won't be enough by itself," Tito remarked. "The farmers and ranchers have proven in the past that they'll fight."

"Won't be no picnic," Bunion said. "Got himself four bindle stiffs that come straight from a prison gang, tough Irish jokers that look to be the kind who live to drink and fight. Besides them filing for homesteads adjacent to his Black Diamond ranch, he has three or four gunmen on his payroll and a foreman who is probably wanted by the law in a half-dozen states."

"That's bad news for the ranchers and farmers."

"Figure there will be some real trouble, if Hytower tries to go ahead with the building of a dam."

"I'd say this load of explosives means he is serious."

"Yup," Bunion rubbed the end of his bushy beard. "There have been a couple engineers around town for the last few days. They've spent a lot of time looking over the river and working on some ideas for Hytower. He means business."

"I've got to get my load delivered out to the old Renikie place." Tito turned back to the business at hand. "My concern is not what any of this stuff is to be used for, only to sign it over to Hytower."

Bunion winked at Luke. "Sounds like you, the last time you showed up in Broken Spoke, don't he?"

"Toughest assignment I was ever given for Wells Fargo," Luke admitted, but then added, "until I was appointed to the position of agent."

"You give that up?" Bunion wanted to know.

"Might say I wasn't cut out for the job."

"There's a young lady hereabouts that will be interested in knowing you're in town. Or are you going to head up that way and surprise her?"

Luke felt a swarm of bees buzzing about in his stomach. "I'll get around to it, soon as I get up the courage."

Bunion chuckled. "You don't think she might be a trifle vexed about you not sending for her?"

"A trifle vexed? I'd say she is probably ready to roast my hide over a bed of hot coals."

"I'm for a bite to eat," Tito said. "Then I'm going to take the wagon up and get rid of my cargo. With luck, I'll make it before dark."

"I'll go along with the bite to eat," Bunion said. "Who's buying?"

"My treat," Luke offered. "The Chinaman still doing the cooking over at the Ace High?"

"Yep, and he's added a number four to his menu."

"Number four?" Tito asked. "That wouldn't be something fine, like maybe a Mexican dish?"

"Don't know what kind of plate he serves it on, but it's pieces of meat mixed in with noodles and flavored with some kind of sauce."

Luke elbowed Tito. "Now you know exactly what to expect."

"Yeah," Tito said dryly, "Maybe I'll let the roulette wheel determine what I order."


Luke had cleaned the plate on a Number Three meal, when John Fairbourn entered the saloon. He spied the three of them at a table and came over to join them.

"Didn't know you were back in town, Mallory," he said, extending his hand. "Been a spell."

Luke shook the man's hand. "Sounds like you've got the pot boiling again, Fairbourn."

John spun a chair around and sat down. "Never a dull moment around Broken Spoke, that's a fact."

"What about this new fellow, the one who wants to be big dog in the pack?"

"He's formed what he calls the Black Diamond Corporation, a cattle ranch and several supporting farms. He's got money, guns, and is using the land grant laws to take legal control of nearly six square miles of property."

"That's quite a chunk of real estate. What are you going to do?"

"I've been over talking to Cartwell Devine. You remember that he is something of a judge."

"Saloon owner, mayor and Sunday bible thumper too, as I recollect."

"He tells me everything is legal, to this point."

"What about the dam? Can he do that?"

"I don't know yet. Cart is going to get in touch with the territorial governor and do some checking for me. I'm thinking it is unlawful to restrict the natural flow of a creek. Especially one that a number of farmers are already using to irrigate their crops."

"You're not here to stop me from taking my cargo up to the Black Diamond are you, John?" Tito asked. "If I remember, you tried to talk Mallory out of delivering his load of barbed wire last year, when he brought it to Broken Spoke."

"Talk?" Luke said, rubbing his chin. "I can still feel the impact from his words."

"Not that I couldn't stop you physically, Tito," John said with a tight grin, "but you are not the enemy here. If I heard the story right, you took up for us the last go-round."

Tito also grinned. "Glad to hear it, Fairbourn. Not that I couldn't handle you, but I hate fighting on a full stomach."

"I've talked to the other cattlemen and Jack Cole, he's still town marshal. If you have a mind to stay around a spell, we're going to have a meeting Friday evening at Cartwell's place. You're welcome to come."

"Welcome by everyone?" Luke quizzed him meaningfully.

"You best be prepared for more of a beating than I gave you, Mallory. Timony is slow to rile, but when fired up, she has something of a temper. I suppose you realize that you've been real careless about keeping on her good side.''

''I've got a fast horse you can borrow,'' Bunion joked. ''That way, if she takes after you with a gun, you can get away quick.''

''You ought to write her a note instead,'' Tito joined in the heckling. ''Better for her to burn the letter than to set fire to your britches.''

Luke groaned. ''What a couple great pals I have.''

John stood up. ''I'm heading out to see a couple of the farmers. If you get bored, you can always help pass the word about Friday night, Mallory. We have to get the support of both the ranchers and the farmers, if we're going to have any clout against Hytower. I'll look for you at the meeting.''

''I'll try to be there.''

John started to leave, but paused, looking back at Luke. ''Good to have you back in Broken Spoke, Mallory. I mean that.''

''Thanks, John. I hope I can convince your sister to feel the same way.''

''Can't promise you anything on that score. You're on your own.''

Once John had left the saloon, Tito also stood up. ''Time to get rid of my cargo, Mallory. I'll be saying good-bye to the both of you.''

''You heading back to Cheyenne when you finish?'' Bunion asked.

''Unlike Mallory here, I still have a job.''

''I was hoping you'd stick around a couple days and maybe go to that meeting with me Friday.''

Tito showed him a tight smile. ''Asking for my gun to side the locals against this Black Diamond bunch, or is it only to prevent Timony Fairbourn from kicking your tail up around your shoulders?''

''Maybe a little of both.''

''I'll see you, Mallory,'' he said, not offering an answer to the question. ''You too, Bunion.''

Bunion waved a hand, but waited until Tito was out of the saloon to speak. ''I remember that we both owe our lives to that man. If he hadn't come to save our bacon, when we faced off against the Renikie boys, you and I would be in the local bone yard.''

''He's a good man,'' Luke said. ''You know, he's never brought the subject up, never even told the story to anyone that I know of.''

''Up till that fight, I always figured him to be just another man who lived by his gun.''

''We were both wrong about him, but how about his new gent?''

''Preston Hytower don't make no beans about his ambitions, Mallory. I figure he's out to take over the world, and Broken Spoke is only his starting point. He has laid the groundwork for a massive house, one that will rival the governor's mansion in most states. He has ordered brick from Colorado to build with, and receives shipments most every week from back east, imported furniture and clothes. Wait until you see his spouse, prettiest thing you ever saw, and he dresses her up like a little store-bought doll or something. He don't seem to treat her like a wife, more like she's something grand for him to show off, 'bout the same as a prize horse.''

''I've seen his kind before.''

''I only spoke to her once, when I had to mend a cracked wheel rim on their barouche. She strikes me about as gentle and sweet as a lamb.''

"Think she married him for his money?"

"Don't seem the sort, but I sure can't think of any other reason."

"Wonder if I can get the lend of my old room, over at the jail?"

Bunion chuckled. "There ain't no one in the cell at present—lessen you count Cole's cat."

Luke uttered a pronounced sigh. "You mean the mangy critter isn't dead yet?"

"I expect you about broke her heart when you left, but she's still there, piles of hair, fur balls and all, waiting for you."

"Wish someone would build a hotel in Broken Spoke. Real shame what a man has to go through for a bed in this town."

Yarrow entered the room and removed his hat. Cassie rose from the table and hurried to get another plate. She loathed having to allow a man she despised share their meals. It was hard enough to keep Preston happy without Yarrow coming around to torment her.

"I've been having Quanto keep an eye on John Fairbourn," Yarrow told Preston, while, as always, he ignored Mont. "The fellow has been about as busy as a bee in a field of flowers."

"Sit down and tell me about it."

Cassie spooned a portion of stew from the kettle onto a plate and hurried over to place it on the table. She didn't miss the way Yarrow leered at her. He was like an evil shadow, watching her every move. Sometimes, she was struck by the feeling that the man was undressing her mentally, degrading her with each perverted look. Worst of all, Preston didn't even seem to notice.

"Like I was telling you," Yarrow began, casting an accusing look in Cassie's direction, "after Fairbourn came out here, I put Quanto on his trail. You know that Quanto is proud of being half-Arapaho Indian. He fancies himself as quite a tracker. Claims he can follow a drop of water in a flood and never get wet."

"And?" Preston showed impatience.

"And he says Fairbourn went to a couple ranches and then to see Cartwell in town. He is sure enough arranging a meeting of some kind."

"Sounds as if these people are going to fight back, nephew," Mont surmised. Cassie didn't miss Preston's hard look at his uncle. He hated being called by anything other than his title. Mont had never tried to endear himself to Preston, and occasionally, he would actually speak up against his wishes. He was as close to an ally as she had since moving from her home.

"We expected that," Preston concerned himself only with Yarrow. "What else?"

"Quanto says he met up with the livery man and a couple of teamster types from Wells Fargo."

"Our shipment," Preston surmised again. "If it's in town, they should be delivering it today or tomorrow."

"One of the two men is headed this way with the wagon," Yarrow confirmed part of his conclusion. "Quanto heard the name of the other man—Bunion called him Mallory." He let the name sink in for a second. "If that's right, he's the one responsible for the death of the Renikie boys."

"Ah, yes, the love interest of Miss Fairbourn, the one appointed as an agent for Wells Fargo over at Junction City. He must have finally come for her."

"Maybe so, maybe not."

"Why do you say that?"

"Quanto said the man was traveling with a full war bag, as if he was carrying everything he owned. He took his stuff over to put up at Cole's place."

"You think he's staying?"

"Looks that way."

"More trouble," Mont again plagued Preston. "You might have to actually work to steal these people's land, nephew."

"I'm not stealing anything!"

"Your plans to divert the water certainly seems devious. If you only wanted to build a dam for the good of all who live in Broken Spoke, the people here would probably pitch in and help."

"I don't need you telling me how to run my life or this campaign, uncle."

"Your father was like that," Mont said, waggling his gray head in a negative motion. "No one could tell him anything either."

Preston's facial muscles worked, the news about Mallory causing him some consideration. When he saw that Cassie had sat back down, he snapped at her. "You didn't fill Yarrow's glass, young lady! Where are your manners?"

Cassie jumped at the harsh tone of his voice. She immediately recognized the familiar danger signals. Whenever something went wrong with Preston's plans, he was irate and short-tempered toward her. She quickly jumped up and filled a glass with lemonade.

"I'd rather have coffee, Mrs. Hytower," Yarrow drawled—*after* she had poured and served the drink.

"I'm sorry," she murmured, removing the glass.

"Sometimes I think she doesn't have a brain," Preston complained. "I paid out a fortune to coach and teach her, I've demonstrated proper etiquette for her myself, forced her to do the same chore over and over a hundred times, and still she gets it wrong. It's like trying to teach a frog to dance."

"You should have picked a more cultured slave for yourself," Mont dug in his spurs. "There must have been dozens of them following after you when we lived back east."

Preston glowered at his uncle, while Cassie felt a flush of humiliation rush to her cheeks. With a trembling hand, she removed the coffeepot from the stove and returned to the table. She placed a cup on the table next to Yarrow and began to pour. He showed a nasty smirk and contributed his own insult.

"It's like you've said all along, Preston, breeding will tell in the end. It's right tough to make a silk scarf out of a burlap bag. The girl comes from a family of worthless immigrants. She'll always be a clinker."

Cassie was overcome with loathing. Yarrow was sitting with one hand in his lap, hidden by the tabletop. Every so guilefully, he reached out and placed his hand on Cassie's lower leg! Startled, she jerked back. A stream of hot liquid splashed from the cup onto Yarrow's lap.

"Ye-Cats!" he yelped, scooting back from the table. "You trying to scald off my hide?"

"Cassandra!" Preston roared. "Watch what you're doing!"

"It wasn't me! He's the one who . . ."

"Say howdy! Mr. Hytower," Yarrow quickly drowned out her protest. "I'm afraid your wife is mad at me for telling you about her little visit with Fairbourn.''

Cassie glared at him. ''You know I didn't do anything wrong. You're always tormenting me or making up lies!''

Yarrow showed a sneer. ''Yup, Mr. Hytower, she's been real uppity since Fairbourn came to see her. Maybe you ought to ask her what they talked about.''

''I was only being polite.''

''Oh, I've no doubt you were being real polite.''

''You're taking your spite out on me because Mr. Fairbourn pushed you around.''

Yarrow grinned. ''He sure seemed eager to defend your honor. Maybe there was something going on betwixt the two of you I didn't see.''

''That isn't so!'' she snapped. ''You're evil and filthy minded, Yarrow! I detest the way you manipulate Preston and constantly try to get me into trouble!''

Preston rose to his feet. ''Cassandra!'' his voice boomed within the room. ''I've had enough of your impertinence. Go to your room!''

She spun on him, furious, trying to defend herself. ''You always take his side against me, Preston!''

''Enough of your sass!'' He snarled menacingly. ''Do I need to give you another lesson in obedience?''

She paled under the threat, her own anger converted to a sudden fear. ''No!'' she simmered instantly. ''I'm sorry, I didn't mean to . . .''

''For heaven's sake, nephew, she only spilled a couple drops of coffee,'' Mont took up for Cassie. ''It isn't worth all this fuss.''

''Stay out of my affairs, Mont. You live under my roof as a guest—don't forget it.''

The old man raised his hands in a sign of surrender. "Sure, nephew, whatever you say."

"Cassandra," Preston snarled each word at her, "I said go to your room. We'll discuss your behavior later!"

Cassie put the coffeepot back on the stove. She bestowed an imploring look at Preston one last time, hoping against all odds that he would recant the command. She saw the fury in his flushed face. It warned her of his ugly mood. If he started drinking—

She hurried from the room as Mont said something she didn't hear. Uncle Mont had tried to come to her defense on more than one occasion. However, his concern often worked against her. Preston disliked any interference in his affairs. Uncle Mont's input usually only added to Preston's anger.

After entering the bedroom, she closed the door and sat down on the bed. Her body was shaking, her heart pounding with a dread anticipation. Preston could be vile and brutal at times. Worse, when his temper was unleashed, nothing she could say or do could slake his ire. It had always been like that. Whenever things didn't go Preston's way, he vented his wrath on her.

Yarrow had intentionally caused her to spill the coffee. He was like some sinister harpy, chosen to be her personal menace, always there to harry and badger her, endlessly causing her to suffer from his relentless persecution. She knew he didn't pick on her from spite, it was something more, always directed with purpose. Having seen the desire in his eyes, she knew his ambition was to possess her. His actions and belittling words were all directed toward his goal to make her his own. In the furthermost regions of her mind, she was terrified of his ultimate plan.

The man used Preston's jealousy and suspicious nature to govern his actions. Preston had been incensed when he learned of her speaking privately to John Fairbourn. Now, a new man had come to town, possibly to oppose or thwart his well-laid plans. She knew from past experience that, when Preston loosed his fury, she was the one who suffered the bruises and aches from his ill mood.

"Dear God," she prayed quietly. "Please don't let Preston be angry with me. Please don't let him hurt me again."

## Chapter Five

It was dusk when Tito approached the old Renikie place. At about a hundred yards from the house, he came upon an old man standing guard with a rifle. He halted the team and gave him a look from head to toe.

The fellow was at least sixty years old, with a neat moustache, bright, flinty eyes, and the posture of a proper gentleman. He had a rifle nearby, but offered Tito a smile in greeting.

"How are you tonight, young man?"

"Tired," Tito replied. "Been a long trip."

"You are the Wells Fargo teamster?"

"Yes, sir."

"Carry on," he said, stepping out of the way. But before Tito could strike up the reins, he added, "See that Preston signs for the delivery personally, would you?"

Tito wondered at the request, but didn't ask why, setting the team back into motion. Continuing down the trail, he pulled into the Hytower yard, stopped and set the brake on the wagon. After a few seconds, he heard a man's angry voice from inside the house. Immediately following, another sound reached his ears, that of a woman crying!

"You here with our load of supplies?" a man asked, stepping out of the shadows.

Tito automatically put his hand on the butt of his pistol. "You Preston Hytower?"

"I'm the foreman for the Black Diamond Corporation. I'll take delivery."

The sound of a strap striking flesh came from beyond the door, followed at once by another sob. Tito's gut churned at the thought of someone helpless being beaten.

"So you're not Hytower?"

"I told you, I'm Yarrow, the foreman."

Tito jumped down, pushed by the man, strode to the door, and banged loudly with his balled fist.

"Hey!" the man cursed. "I told you, I'll take delivery!"

"I'm responsible for consigning this wagon load, mister," Tito shot back. "No one takes delivery from me other than Hytower himself. If he don't sign, I don't leave it here!"

Before Yarrow could protest, Tito hammered on the door again. This time, he pounded louder with his impatience.

There was the sound of a man uttering a profanity, but a moment later, the door was thrown wide open.

"What is it?" the man demanded, his face flushed, out of breath, and snarling every word. "What do you want?"

Tito could smell whiskey on the man's breath and noticed he was buckling on his belt. He knew at once that he had been using the leather strap on someone. He bore into the man with a hard, steady gaze, and when he spoke, his words were hedged with crystals of ice.

"I presume you're Hytower."

"Yes!" the man said, huffing. "What's the big idea, banging on my door like that?"

"Sorry to interrupt the fun you were having," Tito did not mask his contempt, "but I've got a load of supplies here, with your name on the delivery slip. You want to sign for it, or do I take it back to town and let you come pick it up?"

Hytower scowled at Tito. "You have a surly attitude, my friend."

"Surly enough to climb on the wagon and head back to Broken Spoke."

"Maybe that wouldn't be as easy as you think," Yarrow spoke up.

Tito measured the foreman with a glance. He oozed confidence, wore his gun as if it was an extension of his arm, and had the eyes of a killer. He expected men to fear him.

Rather than take him seriously, Tito dismissed the challenge with a shake of his head. "I don't get paid to step on every snake I come across, Yarrow. I'm here to make a delivery, not to play games." He turned back to Hytower. "You want this stuff or not?"

"Check the load and call over some help, Yarrow," Hytower ordered his foreman. At the same time, he took up the list and looked it over.

Tito waited for Hytower to sign the order, then allowed several men to unload the wagon. He didn't offer to help.

"I'm told another man came to town with you," Hytower spoke up, after a few minutes, "man named Mallory, the Wells Fargo agent?"

"Used to be. He don't work for them anymore."

"I don't suppose you know why he came back to Broken Spoke."

"He has a lady friend here."

"Miss Fairbourn," Hytower concluded. "Any other reason that you know of?"

Tito didn't like men who thought the world revolved around them. He also had no stomach for any man who would mistreat a woman or child. "I'm not working for a newspaper, mister. You want to know why Mallory is here, you better ask him."

Hytower looked at him again. "The story I heard about the Renikie boys included a Mexican named Tito Pacheco. That would be you."

"I was there."

"Way the tale goes, you saved Mallory's life."

"I killed a couple men who needed killing," Tito admitted.

"Does that mean you'll side with Mallory, if he gets into trouble a second time?"

"Luke Mallory is a friend of mine." He put a sharp gaze on Hytower. "So is the sheep rancher, Mr. Fielding. Two of my cousins work for him. If someone threatens or starts a fight with them, I'll be there to lend a hand. That answer your question?"

"I don't like your hostile attitude, Mr. Pacheco."

"If you don't like the answers, perhaps you should stop asking questions."

Yarrow walked over to join the two of them at the porch. "That does it, Mr. Hytower. The count is complete to the last spool of wire."

"Very good," he answered. Then he cast a sour, red-eyed look at Tito. "You may leave now, driver. And, if you're smart, you won't stick around Broken Spoke."

Tito didn't offer a reply. He went to the wagon, climbed aboard and turned the team around. Without a backward glance, he started the rig for town. When he reached the guard post, the old gent was there to greet him again.

"Thank you for drawing Preston out, young sir," the man spoke. "He is often quite contemptible when he drinks. I could think of no other way to stop his abuse."

The sound of the girl's weeping still echoed in Tito's ears. Through clenched teeth, he said: "Any man who beats his wife ought to be strung up by his own guts!"

"Hear, hear," the old man replied. "Thank you again."

Tito did not stop, using the whip to coax the twelve-mule team into an easy trot. Then he was watching the dark trail, hurrying his way back to town. He felt the need of a drink.


"What do you think?" Yarrow asked, once Tito was too far away to hear his words.

"You're the expert about gunmen."

"He isn't the kind of man to scare. I'd say he's real handy with his gun."

"Have Quanto keep an eye on him. Make sure he heads back to Cheyenne or Rimrock, anywhere away from here."

"What about Mallory?"

"We'll see what he does next. If he came for his girl, he shouldn't be any bother to us. If he starts poking around, we'll teach him to mind his own business."

"We could be in for a harder fight than we thought, if those two throw in against us, Mr. Hytower. The farmers ain't much, except for Dexter Cline. He strikes me as a tough nut to crack. Then there might be some fight in old man Queen and his two boys. Of the ranchers, Fielding has mostly harmless Mexican herders, Von

Gustin has a couple of fair hands, and there are the two Fairbourn boys.''

"If you need more men, hire them.''

"The Herefords are due in early next week. I've got a couple trustworthy fellows arriving with the cattle.''

"And the big herd?''

"Last word was that they are on their way up from Texas, five thousand head. Everything is on schedule, other than your new house. The shipment of bricks from Colorado is going to take longer than expected.''

"Time is not the issue, Yarrow. I only care about results. My father started with a small amount of money and built a million-dollar factory back east. It was his idea, his sweat, and his tenacity which made it succeed. I learned everything from him. He made a fortune with his own hands and left it to me." Preston shook his head, a grim determination on his face. "The only way I can equal the deeds of my father is to make an empire of my own. I won't be satisfied until I have the biggest ranch in all of Wyoming territory.''

"We should be there within a few years. Got to first mix those Hereford bulls with the Texas longhorn stock and build us a big herd of American breed cattle. Once they start to mature, won't anyone have a bigger or better herd this side of Texas.''

Hytower smiled at the thought. "My dream come true, Yarrow. Let's make it happen.''

"We've got what it takes," Yarrow said. "Once we get control of the water, we'll be on our way.''

"The engineers will be ready to outline that little project very soon. I don't want anything to go wrong with my plans.''

''That's why you hired me, Mr. Hytower, to make sure nothing does go wrong.''

''Preston appeared satisfied. ''I'll see you in the morning, Yarrow. Take care of the details with Quanto.''

''Sure thing.''

Preston went back into the house and walked to the liquor cabinet. The bottle was still out, where he'd left it. He took a clean glass and poured himself three-fingers of bourbon. Tipping the glass, he gulped down the entire contents and set the used glass on the counter. The burning sensation went down his throat and warmed his stomach. The fires of hard liquor slaked his thirst, but he still had an empty sensation.

He put away the bottle and looked at the bedroom. For a moment, he suffered a degree of regret. His conscience always bothered him after he had disciplined his wife. He wondered what demon it was inside of him that made him lose his temper with her. Cassandra was habitually as meek and helpless as a month-old kitten. In his heart, he was certain she hadn't done anything wrong behind his back. As for Yarrow, he had purposely baited her at the table. He wondered why the foreman often chose to try and get Cassandra into trouble. What was his motive?

Locking his hands behind his back, he didn't have to search for that answer. He was not blind. Yarrow was mesmerized by the pure enchantment of his beautiful wife. Practically every man who came near her wanted her for his own.

*The fools! What good is having her?* he was angry once more. He owned her body and soul, she was his wife, but he could not force her to love him. From the first time he had seen her, slaving in his father's plant, he knew she would one day be his. For weeks, even months, on end, he had desperately sought to make her return his desire. When all else failed, he had struck a bargain for her hand. She had been young, innocent, and a dutiful daughter, willing to do anything for her family. Their wedding vows were more a contract between buyer and seller. Never man and wife, it was more a master-slave relationship.

He cursed the weakness in him, for having succumbed to the seductive beguilement of her untainted splendor. Marrying her, however, had been a mistake. He should have taken from her what he wanted and then wed one of the more mature women who lusted after him and his fortune. Uncounted dozens of socialites fawned over him and pursued his favor. He could have had a well-bred society wife at his side, one who readily appreciated the omnipotence of his position, a woman who would have enjoyed and even flaunted the luxury and grandeur of the wealth and prestige he provided.

Instead, he had hired tutors to instruct Cassandra in manners and speech, attempting to mold her demeanor to equal her beauty and natural grace. She had acquired poise, but rejected the superior attitudes of a lady of society. It was not in her nature to be a snob, and she was too down to earth to mingle properly within the pretentious circle of the rich and powerful. He despised any kind of failure, and making her his bride had been a failure. No man or woman could dispute Cassandra's incredible comeliness, but she was not the queen he required.

"Cassandra," he spoke without raising his voice.

There was a hurried shuffle from within the next room. The young woman appeared momentarily, a robe wrapped over her nightclothes. Her eyes were still slightly puffy and red from her tears. She padded barefoot across the room to stand within his reach.

"Yes, Preston?"

"I'd like another bourbon."

She hurried to do his bidding, retrieving the bottle from the cabinet and refilling his glass.

"Join me."

It was not an invitation, but a subtle demand. Cassandra hated the taste of liquor. She could not distinguish even the fine and expensive wine from ordinary vinegar. However, she knew better than to refuse. Tipping the bottle, she poured a small portion into a second glass. She presented the fuller one to him.

"I dislike having to be so rough with you." His words were curt, but rang with sincerity. He tipped the glass and drank it down in a three gulps. "I only wish you to be a gracious hostess, to have the refinement of a real lady."

"I understand, Preston," she murmured softly.

He reached for her—she flinched, a reminder to him that he struck her too often—but she did not pull away. His hand rested on her shoulder and he felt her trembling.

"You have all the beauty and grace a woman could desire," he said. "I only wish to instill in you a measure of cultivation and dignity. If I'm a trifle hard on you at times, it is because I want you to excel, to rise above the ragged beggar you were when I found you."

"I know."

He smiled, assured that all was well between them once more. "When the loads of bricks have been delivered, I'll build us the finest house in the country. There

will be an oak staircase, thick carpets on the floor, a
servant to do the cooking and cleaning. I'll get you a
lady's saddle and you can go for rides with me. We'll
have a house party and invite all the most important people in the country to attend. Everything will be as I promise. You'll see, Cassandra.''

"It sounds wonderful.''

"You should be content,'' he frowned at the lack of
conviction in her voice. "I give you the finest dresses
available anywhere; you have perfume from France,
along with the most expensive imported furniture that
money can buy. I even purchased that exquisite porcelain
tub for your baths. I've given you everything I can to
please you.''

Cassandra stared into her glass, afraid to speak. The
wrong word could incur his wrath again.

"What more can I do? What is it you want?''

She took a sip of the distasteful liquid and refused to
meet his demanding stare. Setting the glass down, she
slowly rotated her head from side to side. "There is
nothing I need or want, Preston. I am your wife. I am
satisfied with whatever you provide.''

He didn't relish her answer, but he rationalized that
he had been a little hard on her earlier. He could hardly
expect enthusiasm. With a sigh, he removed his hand
and said: "Go on to bed. I'll be along in a little while.''

Cassandra backed up a step, put down the unfinished
drink, and turned toward the bedroom. She moved gingerly, evidence that she still suffered discomfort from his
use of the strap on her bare back.

*Blast your temper, Preston!* he cursed his lack of control. *You shouldn't have taken a belt to her.* Still, he felt
justified. It was her own fault. She had been socializing

with John Fairbourn behind his back, and she had been imprudent with Yarrow. The lesson had been necessary.

Preston refilled his glass, his spirits raised. He had apologized. Cassandra was still smarting from the severe castigation, but they had a better understanding now. He tipped the glass to his lips and took another drink. Everything was under control and going as planned.

## Chapter Six

Luke was sitting on the jail cell cot, occupying his sleepless mood by picking cat hairs off of the blanket. Jack Cole's cat, Harlot, had come calling a little earlier, but he hadn't given her enough affection to satisfy her endless thirst for attention. She had gone off after a few minutes to prowl the streets of town. Harlot hadn't changed since his last visit. She had the appearance of a half-sheared sheep, mangy and scruffy, missing bits of fur and leaving hair with about every other step.

As for Cole, he and Bunion were over at the saloon, sitting in at a weekly checker game with a couple other older gents from town. Luke had thought he might catch up on his sleep, but it was not in the cards for him. His eyes burned, longing for a few hours of rest, and his body was stiff and ached from hours aboard a hard wagon seat. He had become soft and out of condition from sitting at a desk. But even though he needed and wanted sleep, he couldn't shut off his brain activity.

He had considered returning to Broken Spoke for months, but under different circumstances. His intention had always been to either send for Timony or come and get her in person. Now, he had no job, no future, no plans beyond each passing moment. He was without purpose, lost, unable to determine where he was going next or what he was going to do. How could he face the girl he loved when he had nothing to offer?

The door to the jail opened and closed. Luke assumed it was Cole returning from the checker game, until a small frame filled the doorway to the jail portion of the small building.

"Timony!" he gasped.

"Luke Mallory!" she hissed the name. "You worthless, low-down, gutless, yellow dog!"

"Timony," he said a second time, as he stumbled up onto his bare feet, "I know how you must feel, but—"

"Don't you dare patronize me! You have no idea how I feel!"

"I . . ."

" 'I'll send for you,' you said!" she snapped the words crisply, storming into the room. " 'I love you! I'll be back for you!' "

He took a step in her direction and helplessly threw up his hands. "Let me explain!"

But Timony reached out and shoved him with both hands, pushing him back into the cell. "You don't have to explain anything! I'm not stupid! I know when I'm not wanted."

"You're wrong about that," he tried to get in a word. "I—"

She pushed him a second time, both tight little fists striking him in the chest. His legs struck the edge of the cot and he sat down abruptly. Timony hovered above him, the hurt and anger flooding her pretty features. "Do you know how people have laughed at me behind my back? Do you care?"

"Of course, I care!"

"All these weeks, I've lain awake at nights and won-

dered if you were all right, if something had happened
to you. I spent endless hours worrying. I rode into town
a hundred times to check for mail. Every time the stage
arrived, I was here to meet it.'' She glared at him, her
eyes filled with fire. ''And what did I get for my trouble?
Saddle sore and a nice long ride back home with
nothing!''

''I didn't know what to say, Timony,'' he jumped at
her taking a breath. ''I couldn't ask you to come join
me. I didn't have time to even sleep.''

''Don't shovel that garbage at me!'' she shouted. ''If
you wanted to be rid of me, you only had to write a
letter saying so. I'm a big girl. That would have been
easier to understand than the way you simply stopped
writing. I thought you had more guts than to shun me
like I was a leper or something!''

''I was afraid you wouldn't understand.''

''You're dead right on that count, you sniveling black-
guard! I didn't understand!''

There was an old adage, *When all else fails, go with
the truth*. Luke took on a serious mien and met her anger
head-on. ''The job was a failure,'' he blurted out. ''I
was a failure! I had my chance at the dice table of life
and I threw snake eyes.''

''Talk sense.''

''I was dismissed,'' he admitted weakly. ''I couldn't
do everything myself, so I trusted another person with
the transfer deposits. She took me and Wells Fargo for
five or six thousand dollars.''

''Oh,'' she displayed not the slightest bit of sympathy,
''so you didn't want me to come and work at your side.
It might have been too much for my little brain. But you

were willing to trust someone else with the company money—and she robbed you blind!''

''Timony, I . . .''

''Stop calling me by my first name, *Mr. Mallory!* You no longer have my permission to be that familiar.''

Luke tried to rise up from the cot, but Timony put firm hands on his shoulders. ''No you don't, you fast talking gigolo,'' she grated the words through her clenched teeth. ''I'm not letting you get in a position to try and put your hands on me. I was overwhelmed by you once, but that was a lifetime ago. You can forget about me ever falling into your arms again.''

''Miss Fairbourn,'' he tried to reason with her, ''listen to me. I wanted to send for you or come back and get you. I've thought of nothing else since I left Broken Spoke. Having you on my mind probably added to the reasons why I couldn't handle the job.''

''How low can a man get, stooping to using me as an excuse for your failure!'' She swatted him smartly on the cheek. ''That's for making me the joke of the valley!''

''But . . .''

''Don't but me!'' She scalded him with her acid words. ''You could crawl over a field of broken glass, on your hands and knees, saying I'm sorry, and I wouldn't take you back now, Mr. Mallory. I'm through with you!''

''Wait a minute. Don't . . .''

''And I better not catch you coming out to our ranch. The next time I see your worthless carcass, I'll darn well fill it with a load of buckshot!''

Luke searched desperately for a way to bridge the icy gap between them, but there was nothing he could say that would combat Timony's fury. She whirled about, strode smartly from the room, and slammed the door upon her exit. He was left with a vast emptiness in his chest, a huge black hole where his heart had once been.

"Dad gum, Luke," he muttered aloud, "lost your job and now your girl. You're definitely on a cold streak."

John was up when Timony came in from putting up her horse. He was sitting in the leather-bound easy chair, with a cup in his hand.

"Got some coffee on the stove," he offered.

Timony was still fuming inside, but she sensed that her brother had something on his mind. While Billy and she talked and teased one another constantly, John was more aloof. He had the responsibility of managing the payroll, hiring men during roundup, directing the work, seeing to it the cattle were tended and everything else associated with running the ranch. He was soft-spoken, very slow to rile, yet was very capable in an argument or actual fight. As head of the Ranchers' Association, he commanded respect from his peers and was well-liked by most everyone who knew him. As for their personal relationship, she had always considered him more of a second father, rather than an older brother.

"I'm not much for coffee this late, John." She waited, but he didn't offer anything more. "Shouldn't you be in bed at this hour?"

"I was waiting to see that you got home all right."

"Probably more concerned if I'd end up in jail for shooting a certain Wells Fargo agent."

He smiled. "As you have returned, I assume you either made good your escape, or you didn't take your gun with you."

She crossed to the stuffed couch and sat down. The turmoil inside of her was like a raging inferno. She hated the ache in her heart, the way she could think of nothing but Luke. Venting her hurt and anger by telling him off had seemed a good idea, but she had to wonder if ending up in his arms wouldn't have been more rewarding.

"Do you think I was wrong to go to him?"

"He had the better part of the day to come see you first," John reasoned. "I'd say he hadn't worked up the courage to make the trip yet."

"If you loved a woman, would you be afraid to face her?"

Something odd took place, a strange expression crossed John's face and he lowered his eyes. Timony could not remember John ever being cowed by a mere question. She waited, studying a reaction that was totally out of character for her self-reliant brother.

"I went to see Preston today, but he wasn't home. He . . ." John leaned back and took a long sip of the coffee. "His wife answered the door."

"Cassie Hytower?"

His head bobbed slightly to affirm her conclusion. "I'll tell you, Timony, she is as pretty as a bed of roses with the charm of a newborn baby. I've never seen any-one with such beautiful brown eyes, soft and radiant, like those of a fawn."

Timony might have laughed at him using such a de-scription, but he was too serious. He had never before confided anything so personal to her. She held her breath and waited, perceiving the fact that he was seeking her counsel.

John hesitated a moment, then blurted, "I don't think she is happy being married to Preston."

"Why do you say that?"

"Just a feeling." He lifted one shoulder in a shrug. "It was nothing she said, only the way she seemed uncomfortable when I called her Mrs. Hytower—and I'm pretty sure the swine mistreats her."

"You think he beats her?"

"Could be. She acted as if she was frightened to death of him."

"A good many men consider discipline as part of their husbandly duties."

"That's hogwash!" he was immediately incensed. "No one has a right to beat their spouse."

"I most certainly agree, John."

He leaned forward again, as if unable to sit still. "You know more about how a woman feels than I do, Timony. Why would a pretty young woman marry a man like him?"

"Preston is a handsome, well-groomed, gentleman. She might have also been seeking a man with self-assuredness and confidence."

John looked her square in the eye. "You didn't state the obvious, the fact that Preston is a very wealthy man."

"You met Cassie. If you had thought she had married for money, you wouldn't be giving her a second thought."

"You think so, do you?"

"I know you, John. You're a man of too high scruples to be interested in that kind of woman."

He laughed without humor. "You say I have scruples, yet here we are, discussing my infatuation with a married woman. Talk about a contradiction in logic."

"What are you going to do?"

John set down the cup, stood up and turned his back

to her. She watched him, fighting an inner war with his conscience and good sense. He was not the sort to allow himself to be tempted by another man's wife, yet he was.

"I don't know, Timony. What can anyone do?"

"Do you think she was forced to marry him?"

"That isn't the issue here. It's a sin to lust after a married woman," his shoulders drooped, "but I can't get her out of my head. I've never felt this way before. I keep seeing the look in her eyes, hearing the softness in her voice." He doubled his fists. "Then I remember how scared she looked, when Yarrow rode in and caught her talking to me. She hates that two-bit gunnie, I can see that much."

"Sounds as if she has good taste—she dislikes Yarrow and likes you."

"It still doesn't explain why she married Preston."

"Are you going to try and see her again?"

"No."

"She will likely continue to attend the Sunday meetings."

John spun around to face Timony once more. "I can't allow myself to feel this way. It's wrong!"

"I know exactly how you feel, John," Timony told him gently. "Believe me."

The frustration slipped from his features. "I'm sorry, kid," he was suddenly back to being her father image, "I'm unloading this on you, while you're probably feeling ten times worse than me. It had to be tough facing Mallory. What did he say?"

"That he wanted to succeed at the job first, before he sent for me."

"Pretty lame."

"And he ended up losing the job anyway. I guess that's why he came crawling back to Broken Spoke."

"What was his excuse for not even writing you?"

Timony felt the flush of embarrassment. "I was so angry, I didn't give him a chance to explain very much. I mean, he hadn't sent a word in almost three months. Does that sound like love to you?"

John lifted both hands, palms outward, as if to surrender. "Don't ask me about love, little sister. I've never even kissed a woman."

She wrinkled her brow. "I know better than that. You remember that I caught you kissing that little señorita from Fielding's ranch after the Fourth of July dance a couple years back."

"She was not a woman yet."

"Oh, so now you're a judge of when a girl becomes a woman?"

"For some."

"What about me?"

He displayed a good-natured grin. "You're about there. Maybe another . . . oh, two or three years."

"What?"

"You've still a lot of growing to do."

Timony hopped to her feet and lifted her small fists. "Oh, yeah?" she challenged, taking up a fighting posture. "I'll show you who is a woman!"

John began to duck and weave. "All right, *Timmy*," he said, snickering, as she frowned at the hated nickname. Then he put up his guard, "I'm ready for you . . . but no thinking about Mallory. That would give you an unfair advantage."

Timony tossed out a few soft punches, missing most of them. The others bounced harmlessly off her brother's arms. John waited for an opening, then he grabbed hold of her hands, spun her around, and wrapped her up like a steer for branding. Before she could get loose, he tossed her onto the couch. Her hair flew from the exertion and came down to cover most of her face. She sat up, blew at the strands of hair and put her hands on her hips.

"Do you give?" she asked, "Or do I have to give you more of the same?"

John chuckled, "Uncle, you win."

"Then you won't call me Timmy again?"

"No."

"And you won't mention Luke Mallory?"

"Not unless you do."

She used one hand to pull the hair from her face. "Okay, you can go to bed now."

"Thank you for your permission."

"And John?" she stopped him before he could leave the room. When he paused to look back, she instilled a serious expression. "Thanks for confiding in me. Anytime you want to talk to someone, I'm more than willing to be here for you."

"Yeah, I know."

"Good night."

He raised a hand in farewell. "See you bright and early in the morning, little sister."

Timony rinsed out John's coffee cup and decided the coffee could be added to and warmed for the morning. After turning off the lamp, she went to her own room. There was a half-moon out, and it filtered a dim glow into the room. As such, she didn't bother to light her lamp, but quickly changed into her night dress and slid under the covers.

Having John interested in a woman was an event for which she had been waiting a long time. It was a disappointing choice, his being attracted to Preston's wife. John was as righteous and decent as any man Timony had ever known. She knew he would never willingly allow himself to feel yearnings for another man's wife. If Cassie had enticed him with her feminine wiles and doe-like eyes, she was something pretty special.

Within the darkness of the room she attempted to beckon sleep. Her eyes would close, but the image of Luke Mallory returned to haunt her. She could not get the man out of her head. It was a conspiracy against her, a diabolical curse. The course of events ran through her brain over and over. She found herself wishing Luke had behaved differently. Perhaps, if he had begged her forgiveness and taken her into his arms he could have smothered her anger with a loving kiss. It might have happened, but she hadn't given him any chance to defend himself. When she took time to reflect upon his being in town, she wasn't even sure if she was the reason for his return to Broken Spoke.

"Oh, thanks a heap for thinking on those lines, Timony," she mumbled under her breath. "It makes me feel so much better!"

## Chapter Seven

Jack Cole leaned on his cane and stood at the cell door, awaiting an answer. When Luke had trouble thinking, he thumped the cane on the wooden floor. "Hey! You got cotton in your ears, sonny? I asked if you was sticking around another day or two?"

"If I have anything in my ears, it's cat hair. How do you stand to be around that scraggly, four-legged hair factory?"

"Yuh don't want to be bad-mouthing Harlot, not when you're a guest in her house."

"Maybe I can get room in Bunion's hayloft."

"Mice have overrun his barn. You don't see no mice here."

"There might be dozens of them, all slinking about under the carpet of Harlot's hair. You can't see them because they would have to walk on stilts to get their heads above the pile of cat hair."

"There yuh go again, picking on a poor, defenseless cat."

Luke took a moment to buckle on his gun. "What about this water project, Cole? Are you going to stand by and let Hytower shut off the water to the valley?"

"I ain't got no say in it. Cartwell has sent a wire to the governor's office, asking about the legal end of it.

Only trouble I see there is Hytower being on a first-name basis with the governor. If there ain't no law against what he has in mind, there won't be any way to stop him.''

"It can't be legal to take water from the existing ranches and farms.''

"Not right, maybe, but legal stuff don't never take the right or wrong of anything into account. If he has the money behind him, that's probably all the right he's going to need.''

"What are the locals going to do?''

"I don't know, Mallory. You remember when you brought in barbed wire last year, how there was the feeling that a war was brewing?''

"Yeah, I remember.''

"The storm warnings are out again, dark clouds that are likely to turn into gunsmoke. I got to tell you, I ain't no younger than when you was here last. If it comes to shooting, about the only thing I can do is duck for cover.''

"You'll pardon me for saying so, Cole, but that's not much of a plan.''

"What I need is a couple deputies. You and Tito done good the last time.''

"But Tito is a teamster for Wells Fargo now. He won't be sticking around.''

"What about you?''

"I haven't decided.''

"You got to vindicate yourself in the eyes of your girl. I can't think of no way better than to take her side in this battle and help.''

"Getting killed is not my idea of how to win back a girl's affection.''

"Dag nab-it! You're getting soft."

"Give me a few days to work this out, before you offer me a job. I'll poke around a bit and get a feel for what's going on."

"I'd feel better if Tito was sticking in town. You make a good target for people to shoot at, but he's the one who can shoot back."

"And you give me a hard time for nagging on your scruffy cat. I've been in a scrape or two and lived through it, Cole."

"Hey, I never said I didn't want you to pin on a badge. You only got to say the word and I'll turn this whole mess over to you."

Luke picked up his hat and paused to remove a long yellow hair from the brim. He gave a hard look at the number of cat hairs on his trouser legs. "I'll be back later. I'm going to borrow a horse from Bunion and take a ride."

"Be careful that you don't get too close to the Fairbourn ranch. Wouldn't want Timony to salt your hide with a load of buckshot."

"Thanks for reminding me."

Stepping out into the spring morning, Luke paused to check the sky. There were a few clouds, some hanging low over the distant hills. A cool breeze was blowing from out of the north and there was a slight scent of a possible storm. The last clouds had come and gone without a drop of moisture. Even so, Luke made a mental note to take his oil slicker, in case it did start to rain. Then he went down the street toward the livery. He wished he could rationalize that he didn't have to involve himself in the troubles at Broken Spoke, but his heart was here. After losing his dream of working for Wells

Fargo there was only one other thing that mattered. He had to win back the heart and trust of Timony Fairbourn.

Dexter paused from his planting to walk over and meet the approaching rider. It was John Fairbourn. He rode as far as the wire fence that protected the crops from grazing Fairbourn cattle and stopped.

"John," he greeted him.

"How's it coming, Dex?"

"Hope I get everything planted before the next rain. It would be nice to have a wetting down after sowing."

"I suppose you know why I stopped by."

Dexter bobbed his head up and down. "Black Diamond."

"A wagon full of explosives arrived yesterday. Tito Pacheco paid a visit up to his cousins—you know the two of them who work for Fielding—and he told them about it. Bernardo came by my house this morning to let me know."

"What are you going to do?"

"This isn't only a problem for the cattlemen, Dex. You know that any sort of dam and Hytower's use of irrigation might alter the flow of the creek or dry it altogether during the late months of summer."

Dexter sighed. "Why does it have to be this way, John? All I ever wanted to do is grow and nourish both my crops and children. I thought we'd seen the last of trouble when we finally put fences around our crops to protect them from your cattle."

"I did too. Hytower took us by complete surprise."

"Have you got a plan worked out?"

"Not yet. I've been trying to pin Hytower down, get him to explain what he has in mind. If he intends to take complete control of our water, we'll have to figure a way to change his mind.''

''Somehow, I don't think he's too worried about what we think. Rumor is, his father was one of those eastern tycoons, the kind who built up his fortune on the backs of women and children working in unheated factories. Paid them nothing, while he was amassing a pile of money for himself.''

''I've heard the same thing, Dex. Can't expect Preston to have much compunction himself with that kind of upbringing. It appears his only interest is in how rich and powerful he can become. The man aspires to be a king.''

''I've spoken to some of the others, John. Even though a dam might be a good idea for the future of Broken Spoke, we'll support any legal moves to halt Preston's plans. If he ends up in control of the Dakota Creek, it for sure won't benefit anyone but him.''

''Glad you recognize him for the snake he is.''

''Thing is, what can any of us do?'' Cline asked. ''Cartwell told me a while back that before Preston moved into the valley, he stopped and made friends with the governor. He knew his actions were going to cause some friction. The man calculates his moves.''

''I intend to confront him, before it comes to a fight. If I can get him to sign some kind of agreement, so we have a mutual say in the water flow, there won't be a problem.''

''He had those four Irishmen stake land and put up hovels to comply with the homesteading laws. He's also got a couple men starting to plant a few trees, just enough to conform with the Timber Act. I don't think he'll be listening to anything you have to say, let alone put his name down on a paper that would take away some of his authority.''

"I suspect you're right, Dex, but I've got to make the effort.''

"Good luck to you, John. I think you'll need it.''

John turned his horse and rode away. Dexter watched him, until he heard the approach of steps behind him. He looked over his shoulder to see Leta, his oldest girl approaching. She had a tray with a pitcher and three glasses. Her face showed her disappointment.

"I thought it might be William,'' she admitted. "John and he look alike from the distance.''

"How nice that you were thinking of me too,'' Dexter said dryly. "I could use a drink.''

"You know I was thinking of you too, Father,'' Leta replied. She stopped and steadied the tray with one hand, while she poured a glass of lemonade with the other. She handed the container to Dexter and showed her disappointment in her voice. "It's just that William hasn't been by since Dawg and he had their fight.''

"He's probably tied up taking care of the ranch, what with John riding about trying to get everyone organized against the Black Diamond bunch.''

Leta sighed. "I wish he was a little more like John, you know, with some of his maturity.''

"He's still a nonchalant kid,'' Dexter said, without a hint of condemnation. He took a long drink, and continued. "At least, he has John as an example, and Timony is a pretty solid gal. He'll learn, given time.''

"I don't want to end up an old woman, while waiting for him to grow up.''

"There are other men around, Leta,'' Dexter put a

steady look on her, "and a good many would like to come courting."

Leta smiled at him. "Yes, only William is the one I want, Father. He might be immature, irresponsible and too carefree at the moment, but he's the one who stirs my heart."

Dexter felt a tenderness for his daughter. He couldn't recall her ever speaking to him in such a direct manner before. He tipped the glass once more, took a couple swallows, and then said: "Like I said, he'll come around one day soon."

"Did you and mother have it, the feeling that you were meant for one another?"

For a moment, Dexter stared off into the distance, recalling the first time he'd looked upon Helen. She had been seventeen, a shy, reserved young lady, with her hair mostly pulled back, except for fashionable curls dangling down in front of her petite ears. He had fancied those curls looked like glossy black ribbons, decorating the dainty features of her modestly attractive face. The first time he had caught her eye, he knew she was interested in him.

"I think you could say we were drawn to one another, Daughter. Once I met your ma, I never wanted another woman. I like to think she was attracted to me in the same way."

"That's the way I feel about William," Leta said. "I'm pretty sure he had the same feelings. Far as I know, he hasn't tried to court any of the other girls in Broken Spoke."

Dexter finished the drink and handed the glass back to Leta. "Then I suppose you'll have to wait him out, give him another year or two to mature."

Leta's chest heaved with another sigh. "You're probably right, Father, but it doesn't make it easy—the waiting, that is."

"Thanks for bringing out the lemonade . . ." he grinned, "even if it wasn't for my benefit."

Leta patted his arm. "You'll always be the first man in my life, Father. I would have brought out the lemonade anyway."

He watched her turn around and start for the house. His heart swelled, thinking of Helen, Leta, and his three other children. It was an awesome responsibility, providing for and directing the lives of his wife and children. He couldn't allow anyone to ruin the lives they had, and that included Preston Hytower and his Black Diamond Corporation!

Luke looked at the three men who made up the Queen family with a sense of annoyance. Why did he continue to waste his breath?

"It will take a united effort by everyone in the valley, if we are to stop Preston Hytower from using a dam to control the water to Broken Spoke. If he should decide to reroute the stream, your farm will dry up and blow away."

Miller spat a stream of tobacco juice into the dust. "Ain't no one going to stop our water, Mallory. Me and my boys will see to that."

"Hytower has hired himself some guns. One is from Texas, goes by the name of Yarrow. I imagine there are a half-dozen or so working for him that wouldn't back off from a fight."

"We ain't no one to back off either," Dory Queen piped up.

''That's right,'' Chad Queen also joined in. ''If it's a
fight that thar eastern dude wants, we'll shore enough
accommodate him.''

''Look, I don't have a personal stake in this, but I
don't want to see another war come to Broken Spoke.''

''You sure enough hauled the last one to our door,''
Miller sneered. ''It was you what done brung in the
barbed wire.''

''I know.''

''What's your interest in this anyhow?'' Chad asked.
''You don't live in Broken Spoke.''

''I've friends here.''

Dory laughed out loud. ''He means that wildcat from
the Fairbourn place, Miss Timony! I recollect that's what
got you mixed into the fight against the Renikie boys.''

''There's going to be a town meeting,'' Luke ignored
his remarks, ''Friday night, about dusk, at Cartwell's
courthouse. At least one of you should attend to repre-
sent your interests.''

''We'll consider it,'' Miller said thickly. Then he spat
again into the dirt. ''Now, why don't you just git?''

Luke neck-reined his horse around and put the mare
into an easy cantor. The Millers hadn't changed. They
were still stubborn and suspicious of everyone. Worse,
they figured they could handle any situation by simply
taking up their guns and wading into a fight. Tito had
told him about meeting Yarrow at Hytower's place. If
Tito was heedful of the man, it stood to reason that he
was the sort you gave a wide path.

Reaching the fork in the trail, Luke glanced off to the
east. There was Fielding's sheep ranch and the Fairbourn's Rocking Chair ranch. He sorely wanted a chance
to make up with Timony, but she would need a cooling-

down period. Attempting to talk to her before she had simmered would be like tossing black powder onto a burning fire.

With a sigh, he pointed his horse to the west and Von Gustin's ranch. He would speak to him, then swing up and also see Big George. If everyone showed from the farms and ranches, there ought to be twelve or fifteen men at the meeting. They had the strength to stand against Hytower, but only if all of them were in it together.

He rounded a bend and jerked his horse to a stop. Three men were waiting for him, two with rifles leveled at his chest!

"What's the idea?" he asked, jerking his horse to a stop.

A man with a scar across his nose spoke first. "You're on Black Diamond range, mister. We don't allow no trespassers."

"This is the main trail between Von Gustin's ranch and town. You mean to tell me that you now own the road?"

"Toss your iron and light down from the horse, Mallory—or die where you sit."

"How'd you know my name?"

The man grinned. "It's our job to know anyone who pits themselves against Black Diamond. Pitch the six-shooter and dismount."

Luke had no chance against three of them. He eased his gun out and let it drop. Then, carefully, he dismounted.

"You don't belong in this valley, Wells Fargo man," the guy sneered. "Maybe you need some convincing to go home."

"I don't know what you're talking about."

The one man who didn't have his rifle out shook out a loop. Before Luke had an inkling as to what he intended, the rope was tossed out and settled around his shoulders.

"Hey!" was the only word he got out.

The man yanked the noose tight. Luke realized what he had in mind, but didn't have time to get loose. The fellow spun his horse and kicked him in the ribs. Luke was pulled off of his feet and landed on his stomach. As the rope was stretched tight, he managed to catch hold of the rope with both hands. Then he was being dragged across the open ground, bouncing off of sagebrush and taking a tremendous beating from rocks and clumps of brush.

The rider took the trail for the first fifty feet, then turned off toward more rugged country. Luke tried to squint through the dirt being thrown up from the heels of the horse. By lunging to one side or the other, he was able to avoid some of the stands of brush or more deadly rocks for the first little way. In a matter of seconds, however, he was blinded by the flying dust. He was then at the mercy of the bounding horse, hammered and jolted each time his body slammed against an obstacle. Like a tin can tied to the back of a wedding wagon, he was tossed and jounced around, lambasted by the hard ground until he was knocked senseless.

The world was black before his eyes, but something penetrated into his unconscious world. He felt himself being shaken and slowly fought to break through from the darkness. Water was splashed into his face and he pried his eyes open, about half cognizant. As he fought to remain aware of his surroundings, a growling voice barked right into his ear.

"This is the only warning you're going to get, Mallory," the man rasped. "Soon as you can sit your horse again, you ride away from Broken Spoke and don't look back."

Luke had a mouthful of dirt, mixed with blood. He was too groggy to offer any reply. In a daze, he was vaguely aware of being hoisted over his saddle. His hands and feet were lashed to the stirrups, then the horse was swatted on the rump.

Jolted with the horse's every bound, Luke could not focus on the swiftly passing ground. His stomach and ribs absorbed the pounding of the saddle, pummeling him unmercifully. In a matter of seconds, he was lost to a second blackness that swallowed all of his conscious thoughts and smothered the agony. His last notion was that he might never wake up again.

Cassie walked in the direction of the window, wondering how to judge the time when Preston would return. She didn't want to start frying steak until she knew how many mouths she would have to feed. The corn bread was cooling and the potatoes were in to bake. The day was warm, so she had the back door open for ventilation. She stopped short, not moving all the way up to the window.

Yarrow was on the front porch, sitting under the shade of the overhang, occupied presently with the chore of biting off a chunk of his plug of tobacco. He used a finger to shove the wad into his cheek, where its bulge made him look like a chipmunk with a mouth full of acorns.

Cassie backed away quietly, filled with revulsion. She glowered at his back, wishing she had the power to strike him dead. How she detested that man. He was a disgusting human being, vile and evil. She hated the way he watched her, following her every move with hungry eyes. He seemed to live only to find ways to tease or taunt her. It was because of him that she had to hang blankets when she took a bath. He was not above spying on her from a window. And his serpent's tongue constantly put her at odds with Preston. He always took Yarrow's side, always accepted the worst about his own wife. She had often suffered abuse and even physical punishment simply because of Yarrow's cruel streak.

Because of their situation, the dependency Preston had on Yarrow, he allowed the man privileges that he would never have given any other man. The gunman came and went as he pleased, insulted and belittled Cassie, and paraded around as if he was the one who owned the Black Diamond. She despised his yellow-brown teeth and bad breath from chewing tobacco, loathed the lecherous smirks, the degrading leer, and the endless snide remarks.

Cassie went into the kitchen and sat down. There was nothing to do but wait. It was always more distressing when she didn't have something to keep herself busy. When working, there was not the time for daydreaming. To have time to contemplate, her brain continually sought fantasies in the sky, venturing into private rooms within her mind to muse how things might have been if . . .

She immediately scolded herself, for the image of John Fairbourn entered her head. She was not so naive that she hadn't seen the wishful craving in his eyes.

When he looked at her, she felt the same yearning. It was wrong. She knew it. She also knew that he knew it. They both knew it, yet it was present, unspoken desires and dreams, immoral, but undeniably present.

Her only escape from her reprehensible existence was in her dreams. She would never violate the promises she had made on her wedding day. No matter how Preston treated her, she was his wife, legally and morally. She hoped that God did not hold her accountable for the day-dreams her imagination occasionally created.

The sound of the carriage reached her ears, plummeting her back to reality. Preston was home. She could start preparing the meat for frying. Engrossed in her work once more, perhaps she could dismiss such libertine notions.

John could smell the aroma of supper cooking from inside the Hytower home. It reminded him that the day was growing late. He knew this stop was a waste of time and energy, but it was something he had to do. He would exhaust all means to prevent a power struggle or actual shooting war.

Preston had seen him approach and came to stand in the door of his house. He offered no hospitality, poised, arrogant, head held high, as if he was the most important man in the world. He listened impatiently, while John made his proposal. Then, haughtily, he gave a negative shake of his head.

"You are wasting your time, Mr. Fairbourn. I am not interested in making concessions about the dam I intend to build. The flow of water will be determined by the amount of rain and snow, and by the tributaries that feed

Dakota Creek. I intend to have the irrigation that I need
for Black Diamond's cattle, grain farms, and timber.''

''There are already existing ranches and farms that
require some of that water, Hytower. You can't move in
here and simply take away those people's livelihood.''

He laughed, as if John's argument was absurd. ''You
don't seem to grasp the situation. Mr. Fairbourn. I'm the
one who owns the most land now.'' With a snide curl
to his lips he added, ''However, I'm a reasonable man.
Once I have the dam completed, I will sell off shares of
water to anyone who desires irrigation. I assure you, the
costs will not be prohibitive to raising a decent crop.''

John held his temper. ''How about if we provide some
of the manpower or raise a portion of the money for the
dam project? We can work together on this. All it would
take is some kind of formal agreement as to the disper-
sion of the water.''

Hytower's eyes gleamed. ''You are not without some
intelligence. I can see you plan to maintain the status
quo here in Broken Spoke, but I'm afraid I'll have to
bow out of such a contract. As you are probably already
aware, I have a sizable herd of cattle headed this way
from Texas. When they arrive, I seriously doubt that any
of you will have enough water to survive.''

''What kind of swindle are you trying to pull?''

The man shrugged his shoulders. ''I wasn't the first
one to come to this part of the country, but I have a
vision that is far greater than any of you small-minded
ranchers. What I see is an endless herd of cattle, a vast
empire that encompasses a couple hundred square miles
of Wyoming territory. When the day comes that we are
admitted statehood, I shall be the most powerful man in
the entire country. I may accept the position of governor,

or I might even use my wealth and influence to run for office on a grander scale.''

''Like President of the United States?''

The grin played on his lips. ''As we don't have a king in this country, I suppose I could settle for that title.''

''You're insane.''

''No, Mr. Fairbourn, only the poor or homeless are insane. As I am a rich man, I'm what is called eccentric.''

''I was hoping we could get along, find some common ground.''

The smile faded and a dark light sprang into his eyes. ''Common ground—like my wife, perhaps?''

There was vicious accusation in his voice, but John did not take the bait. ''You have to make some concessions about the water or you'll end up with a war on your hands, Hytower.''

''Make that *Mister* Hytower, when you speak to me. I'm not one of your toe-headed cowboys or clod-kicking farmer friends.''

John doubled his fists, arms rigid at his sides. For a moment, he felt the urge to take this man on physically, beat him to within an inch of his life and then crush him under the heel of his boot. He resisted the impulse with some effort. It was to his credit, as Yarrow appeared from out of nowhere. He was not fool enough to think Yarrow would settle a difference of opinion with his fists. The man had his hand on the butt of his pistol, and John had the impression it would take little provocation for him to draw and shoot. As John was both the aggressor and on Hytower's land, he had little choice but to walk away.

''You are no longer welcome on my property,'' Preston informed him concisely. "I suggest that you depart forthwith and don't return."

"You're making a mistake, Hytower," he purposely did not put a mister in front of his name. "We aren't going to sit back and whittle sticks while you move in and ruin everything we've built."

"We're patrolling our borders," Yarrow was the one to speak. "Just so you know, trespassers will be dealt with severely."

"Your borders encompass several main trails and the only road between a couple of the ranches and town."

"Looks as if you people will have to find yourselves a new route."

John glowered at him, his jaw anchored, eyes burning into the man. If he thought he had even a slight chance against Yarrow, he would have made a grab for his gun. He was not such a fool, convinced that such an act would have played right into their plans.

"I'm sorry we can't reason this out," he stated. "I hoped there would be some middle ground, a way to compromise."

"This is your leniency trip onto my land, Mr. Fairbourn," Hytower snipped. "The next time you cross onto my property, my men have orders to deal out a measure of harsh punishment."

John mounted his horse and glared down at the two men. "You better take some time and reconsider your plans," he warned. "If you aim to start a war against us, we'll darn well fight back."

"Now, now, Fairbourn," Yarrow quipped, "don't you be scaring us. I won't be able to sleep at night, worrying about you and all those tough guns you can pit against us."

"You're both making a big mistake."

"Yeah, yeah, we know," he grinned, "but what's a fellow to do? You boys don't want to share your toys."

John set his teeth. "It's only a game to you both, isn't it?"

"A game we intend to win," Yarrow answered. "Take your nag and ride out. And," he grew serious, "don't come sniffing around Mr. Hytower's wife again. I catch you at the house a second time, I'll kill you."

"You talk real tough, Yarrow. I'd admire to see how brave you are without a gun on your hip."

He chuckled, the seriousness gone. "You ain't likely to find out."

"I'll be seeing you both again."

"By the way, Fairbourn," Yarrow showed a sinister smirk, "give our regards to Mallory, when you see him, or to whatever is left of him."

John was curious at his remark. Rather than ask for an explanation, he took a last hard look at the two men and started his horse moving. As he put the ranch house behind him he mulled over the words Yarrow had said, *Whatever is left of him.* What did that mean?

John felt the mist. It was not the needed rain the farmers had hoped for. The teasing sprinkle was only a reminder as to how badly the Dakota Creek was needed. There was still hope for a night shower, but the clouds looked to be breaking up. Morning would likely bring a clear sky.

As it was growing late, John turned back for his ranch. He decided to keep the news about Mallory to himself until morning. He would make a trip into town and see what Jack Cole or Bunion could tell him. If something had happened with Mallory, one or both of them would know it. He, along with everyone in the valley, owed Mallory a debt for taking care of the Renikie boys and helping prevent a war over the arrival of barbed wire in Broken Spoke. Besides which, if the ex-teamster had run into trouble, John had darn well better get some answers for Timony. Say what she would about their relationship being over, he knew his sister was still madly in love with Luke Mallory.

## Chapter Eight

It was the next morning when John rode into Broken Spoke, intent upon talking to Cole or Bunion. However, he managed only a single step from where he'd tied off his horse when he spied Cassie Hytower. She was on the porch of the general store, decked out in a charming powder blue dress and perky matching bonnet, poised with a lace parasol over one shoulder. Even as he stared helplessly in her direction, she looked back.

The outside world ceased to exist for him. He saw nothing but her, as if he was standing deep within a cave and could see only the light at the entrance. His brain went from a casual walk to full gallop, as he sought any excuse he could think of for speaking to her. Without giving permission to his legs, he discovered himself moving toward her.

Cassie did not put on a coy act. She rotated about and smiled at his approach. Her greeting was friendly.

"Good day to you, Mr. Fairbourn. What brings you to town?"

John reached up to remove his hat, but it struck him that his hair was unkempt and damp from the hard ride. He altered the action to make an informal touch to the brim in a salutary greeting.

"Hello again, Mrs. Hytower," he replied. "You look mighty pretty in that blue dress."

That put a slight flush into her cheeks. "Thank you," she said.

"Shopping today?"

"Uncle Mont brings me in to check the mail each week and pick up whatever fresh produce they have at the general store."

John managed to tear his eyes from Cassie long enough to glance into the mercantile. He saw the elderly man, neatly dressed in a suit and tie, standing a few feet away. At John's look, he gave him a silent nod.

John made the effort to be friendly. "Howdy, Mont, is it?"

"Mr. Fairbourn," Mont replied without any display of emotion. "Seen you at the house yesterday."

"A less than successful visit it was too."

Mont gave a knowing bob of his head. "Speaking to Preston is like talking to a wall of stone."

"Are you in town to pick up the mail too?" Cassie asked, before they could continue on that line.

"No, my sister has been handling that chore for a spell. Actually, it was something Preston said yesterday that brought me to town. I was on my way to see Jack Cole; he's the town marshal."

She smiled. "Yes, I've spoken to him once or twice," then with a girlish giggle, "and I've seen his tattered-looking cat. It was curled up in a ball next to him; I thought at first it was a pile of old rags."

He felt a wonderful lightness at seeing and hearing her laughter. "I believe the person who thought up the word mangy must have had a cat like Harlot."

She laughed again. "That's the cat's name?"

"Name and reputation both."

"How dreadful."

He chuckled, swept away with her mirth. "Makes a person concerned about how desperate the local toms are in this town."

Cassie's smile faded. "Did you and Preston reach an agreement?"

"Not exactly—more of an understanding."

"The boy is just like his old man," Mont contributed to the conversation. He stepped over to join the two of them. "My brother, Garth, was zealous, single-minded and tenacious. He didn't care about anything or anybody once he set himself on a path to money and power. He raised Preston to think by the same set of rules." He shook his gray head. "I recall the boy walking the assembly lines when he was still in his schooling years. He was reprimanding help and even firing workers by the time he was fifteen. I do believe the boy would have dismissed his own mother, if she had failed to measure up to the company expectations. I saw him bring more than one woman or child to tears. Once he was old enough, he took over a portion of the business and was equally as demanding as his father. They were a matched pair of petty tyrants for years."

"Why did he leave that life to come west?"

"He read about the cattle barons in Texas. I suppose the title of baron sounded more to his liking than being a mere tycoon."

John was surprised at the amount of animosity in Mont's voice. He ventured: "I presume Garth has passed away?"

"Preston sold the business the week after his death, took at least ten percent less than it was worth. A few days later, the house and all properties were sold off too. For several years, before his father passed on, Preston had been researching places where he could become king.'' There was the slight upturn of Mont's mouth. ''He picked Broken Spoke.''

''And he hired those Irish workers to stake land claims?''

Mont grunted. ''Those four men were recruited from a jail cell. He paid their fines and hired them to sit on the land until he could legally claim it as part of his corporation.''

''Under the Homestead Act, that means five years.''

''There is a provision under that act which allows a person to buy the land after as little as six months at $1.25 an acre.''

John was hit with a jolt of reality, as if he had been foundering about in the darkness and someone had struck a match. With a little maneuvering, Preston could end up legally owning the entire six square miles his Black Diamond group had claimed. He would have the water and grazing for his cattle, while his gunmen would repress any opposition. The plan was no longer a threat, it was very real. If Preston was going to be stopped, it had to be now, before he acquired both the water and the land from the four Irishmen.

''Should you be telling me all this?'' he asked Mont.

''Makes no difference to me, son. I'm an old man, living out the last few years of my life alone. If not for the young lady here, I'd have ended up in some kind of boarding house for old people. She convinced Preston that I would be good company.''

''Uncle Mont worked in the office for Garth,'' Cassie informed John. ''He handled the orders and paperwork for the company for twenty-five years.''

''And got pennies for my efforts,'' Mont replied bit-

terly. "Garth kept promising me that he would give me
a promotion, that he would one day make me a partner."
He sighed. "Like I said, Preston and Garth come from
the same mold, both of them as warm and compassionate
as a railroad spike."

"Sounds like you got a raw deal."

"Oh, I made enough to live and had myself a good
life. I was married for over twenty years, but we lost our
only girl to fever and both sons to the war. My bride
passed onto the next world ahead of me—" he thought
for a moment—"been almost seven years now. I look
forward to being with her again."

John didn't know how to respond to something so personal. Mont did not make him uncomfortable for long.
He put his attention on Cassie. "I'll be over looking at
the work gloves. Mine are getting a little worn."

"I'll be right along," she promised. Once he was inside, she again confronted John.

He locked gazes with her, amazed at the sparkle and
life which beamed from within the young woman. Words
were inadequate to compare with the winsome spirit he
deduced was locked behind those rich chocolate eyes.

"I've been hoping I'd run into you again," she murmured softly. "I wanted to apologize for Yarrow being
so rude."

"Man filled with that much hot air is going to end up
bursting his own balloon one day."

"I shouldn't have asked you to come into the house.
Preston is very strict about any visitors."

"After our talk yesterday, he'd no doubt have an apoplexy if he knew you were talking to me here and
now."

"I'm sure of it."

"You aren't one of his cattle or a hired hand, ma'am," John said through tight lips. "A man is supposed to honor his wife. Especially someone like you."

The slight rush of color tinted Cassandra's cheeks again. "It was nice to see you again, Mr. Fairbourn. Again, I must apologize for the behavior of our foreman."

"No apology necessary, Mrs. Hytower, I consider the source."

For no apparent reason, the lady reached forth, as if she desired a personal touch to transmit her unspoken feelings. John did not shake her dainty hand, but he took it for a short moment and held it. In that instant, he was assailed by a host of emotions. A tingle ran up his arm and set his heart to pounding. Somehow, he knew all of his dreams were in that touch, a romance that could never be.

"Good day to you, madam," he managed through the constriction in his throat.

Cassie quickly withdrew her hand, as if suddenly fearful that someone might have witnessed the act. Then she hurried into the store.

John physically forced himself not to gawk after her. He spun on his heel and walked brusquely back toward the jail telegraph office. Jack must have seen him coming, for he appeared out on the porch, before he reached the building. There was a deadly serious expression on his aged and weathered face.

"You hear about Mallory?" he asked John.

"Nothing specific. What happened?"

"Ain't sure exactly. He was on one of Bunion's borrowed horses. The animal come wandering back to the livery yesterday afternoon, with Mallory tied over the saddle. Looked as if he had been dragged over about a mile of jagged rock. He's pretty banged up.''

''Where's he at?''

''Bunion took him in to doctor him. I don't know if he'll pull through or not.''

''I know now what Yarrow meant,'' John rasped. ''That slimy snake gave me a warning, but I didn't understand what he was talking about. I'd say the lines have been drawn into the dirt, wide and deep. It's Black Diamond against the rest of us.''

''Cartwell got an answer about the water. There don't seem to be any rules concerning who has the right to change the flow of a stream. If Wyoming was a state, there might be laws of some kind, but in a territory, we don't have any guidelines to follow.''

''So what alternatives does that leave us?''

''Two possibles, John. One is the oldest rule in the history of the world: *might* is right. It means a fight to settle who controls what. The other possible is that the man who owns the dam is the one with the strings. He does the pulling.''

''Has Tito left for Cheyenne yet?''

''He has, before Mallory come back draped over his saddle. He did leave a message for Mallory, but I ain't been able to give it to him yet.''

''What's the message?''

Cole removed a piece of paper from his pocket. ''Wrote it down, he did,'' he explained. ''I figured it was private, so I only read it once. Let's see,'' he turned the paper right-side up, ''it says 'Hytower plans to dam up the water for his own use.' '' Cole lifted one shoulder. ''No surprise there.''

John looked over at the paper. ''What else does it say?''

''Oh, yeah, he writes that Preston also beats his wife.''

A searing fury roared within his chest. John doubled his fists so tightly it hurt his fingers. He could not mask the rage that swelled inside of him.

Cole folded the paper. ''That putrid maggot!'' he swore under his breath. ''Can you imagine anyone harming that little girl?''

''Tito must have seen or heard something when he made delivery up to the Hytower place,'' John guessed, unballing his fists to prevent cracking the bones in his fingers. ''At least it saves me from a petty dislike. I can hate the sneaky, crooked, power-hungry skunk right off.'' He stared at Cole. ''What are you going to do about it?''

''Do about what? The water?''

''No! The girl!''

''She's his wife. I can't do anything without her making a complaint. I once read about a statute or a law against a man beating his wife, but I ain't never heard of no one using it.''

''What if the woman is too frightened to charge her husband? Do you sit back and wait until she ends up dead?''

''Look, John, we ain't got no real information here. You and I don't even know what Tito's note is talking about. I can't run over to the store and start questioning a woman about her relationship with her husband.''

''There has to be something we can do.''

''Not me,'' he squinted up at John, ''but if you was to somehow get some inside information, you could pass it on.''

"Why tell me? I'm not involved."

"I seen the two of you jaw-boning just now. Are you sure you ain't involved?"

"She's a married woman, Cole."

"Don't mean the two of you can't be friends."

John didn't want to talk about it. "I'm going over to check on Mallory. It's pretty obvious that we're going to need the kind of law like the last time he pinned on the badge."

"I could take offense at that."

John relaxed, "If you don't take offense at having that scruffy cat around shedding a mountain of hair, you won't mind a little thing like blood and guts being spilled."

"What is it, open season on helpless cats? Everyone keeps picking on poor Harlot!"

"Might be a message in that," John quipped. Then he whirled about and headed toward Bunion's place.


Timony heard the voices in the next room and quickly finished her bath. She toweled herself off and quickly threw on her work clothes. Exiting her bedroom, she saw Token and Billy, both sitting at the table with John. There were coffee cups in front of each of them.

"You didn't have to rush your bath, kid," John told her. "We're only having us a cuss and discuss session."

"About what?"

He sighed, aware that she was not going to be left out. "It looks as if Hytower is beginning his move. Big George has had Cully Deeks doing some snooping. Cully spoke with a couple of engineers that were charting the Dakota Creek's course. He came back with bad news.

Preston isn't only thinking of putting in a dam, he is considering a method to alter the flow of the creek.''

She was crestfallen. ''Then we do have trouble.''

''He is going to need the water to make good on the Black Diamond land claims. In a matter of six months, he can buy the land those Irish farmers have staked. He is also bringing in enough cattle to ruin grazing for every rancher in Broken Spoke.''

''How can he do that?'' Timony wanted to know. ''We were here first! The farmers were here before him! Where does he get off coming into the valley and taking over?''

''I say we put together a band of vigilantes and burn him out!'' Token exclaimed hotly. ''We have a right to defend ourselves.''

''I'm with Token,'' Billy agreed. ''The longer we wait, the stronger foothold Hytower is going to get.''

''Fighting and killing can't be the only answer.''

''Wake up, John!'' Token was red-faced with his anger. ''You're the head of the Ranchers' Association. You've got to be the leader in this fight. Do you want us to simply hand over the title to our land, give the man our cattle, get on our knees before the pious self-made king and thank him for letting us keep our lives?''

''I ain't crawling for nobody, John,'' Billy vowed.

John shook his head. ''There has to be a legal way to do this.''

''Legal!'' Token was shouting. ''Is taking our water legal? Is fencing us off of our own land legal? Is beating a man to death legal?''

Timony frowned at his last remark. ''Who was beaten to death?''

The three men were suddenly solemn. Timony looked from one to the other, then stared hard at John. "Well?"

"Some of Hytower's caught a man on their property and dragged him back of a horse, but he isn't dead."

"Not yet," Token grumbled. "You said yourself that he might not make it."

"Who might not make it?" Timony asked, suddenly fearful. "Who was dragged back of a horse?"

John could not meet her inquisitive stare. "Mallory," he barely uttered the name.

Timony was stunned. The strength to stand left her. She was forced to sit down at the table, a great, invisible weight crushing her. The thoughts in her head were too scrambled to sort out. She slowly shook her head back and forth.

"Bunion is tending him," John continued gently. "I spoke to him before I left town. He said he didn't think there was any internal bleeding. Mallory should make it. He's rawhide-tough, kid."

"Why do you think they picked on him?" Billy asked. "He don't have any stake in Broken Spoke," he glanced at Timony, "unless you count his courting sis."

"Maybe it was to make a point," Token suggested. "Take out the one man responsible for ending the fighting last year. What better way to show their power than to eliminate him from the picture."

"It still don't make any sense," Billy reiterated, "not unless Mallory was looking to side us in this here fight."

John put in: "I think he was going to do just that. Cole had already asked him to pin on a badge."

"And did he?"

"No, but he should have. If the Black Diamond bunch

had treated a marshal that way, it would have put them on the wrong side of the law.''

''If he dies, it'll be murder. That puts them on the wrong side of the law no matter what!''

Timony hated the sound of those words. ''He won't die,'' she proclaimed, ''I feel it.''

There was an awkward silence for a few moments. Token cleared his throat and finally spoke up. ''Meeting is tomorrow night in town, John. I reckon there ain't nothing for us to do until we gather everyone together.''

''I'll go along with that,'' Billy added. ''Might as well get to work and pick this up at the meeting.''

John remained at the table while Billy and Token left the room. After a lengthy pause, he placed his hand over Timony's own.

''I saw him, kid,'' he was sympathetic. ''He was pretty banged up, but he had some color. I think he'll be okay.''

''Why do I care?'' she asked, ducking her head. ''He spurned me for over two months! He deserted me! I shouldn't give an ounce of dust whether he lives or dies.''

''I don't think hearts work that way.''

Her eyes lifted and she studied his face. ''You're still troubled by Mrs. Hytower aren't you?''

''Worse, I saw her again today and . . .'' he could not keep the heated passion from entering his voice, ''I also learned that Preston beats her.''

''You saw her at the ranch?''

''No, in town with her uncle. I don't think Mont Hytower likes his nephew very much. He was willing— eager is a better description—to tell me about anything I wanted to know. The rumors are true. Preston has a shipment of Hereford bulls on its way here, and also has a major cattle drive coming up from Texas. We are in a fight for our lives against this man.''

''What about Cassie?''

''What about her?''

''Did she smile at you? Bat her beautiful fawn-like eyes? Try and hold your hand?''

He didn't care for her assessment, especially the fact that she was right on all counts! To hide the truth, he changed the subject.

''You going to visit Mallory?''

''I don't know.''

''He might die.''

''You said only a moment ago that he looked pretty good.''

''No, I said there was some color to his face—other than the black and blue from the battering he took. He was unconscious the whole time I was there. Bunion said he hadn't come to since the horse brought him into the livery.''

''But you don't really believe he would up and die?''

''Do you love him or not?''

Timony could not answer that. She had grown thoroughly irate and lost all patience over the endless weeks of not hearing from him. Then, when he had finally arrived, he had not even warned her ahead of time. Could she love someone as inconsiderate as that?

After a few seconds of internal struggle, she said: ''I ought to ride into town and pick up some things. We are running low on salt.''

''Coffee too,'' her brother supportively contributed to the plan. ''Must be all these late hours we're keeping around here.''

Timony attempted a smile, but failed miserably. "We're a great pair, John. You've a hankering for a married woman, and my feelings are being held prisoner by Luke."

"Hankering? I don't think I've ever heard you use that word."

"Luke once used it to describe his feelings for me."

"No wonder he's won your heart, the romantic devil."

"If I'm not back in time for dinner . . ."

"Token's wife can manage," John finished for her.

"Thanks, John. I'll get my horse."

"Yeah, see you later, kid."

Timony went into her bedroom and quickly changed her clothes. Pausing for a moment, she sank down to her knees and stared up at the ceiling. With her hands pressed together, she closed her eyes.

"Dear Lord," she began devotedly, "please forgive me for the evil thoughts and any sins I might have committed lately. I really want to be a good person." Taking a deep breath, she clasped her hands more tightly. "I'd be very thankful if You would watch over Luke Mallory and help make him better." Pausing, she was at a loss for words. "Bless my brothers, Token and Linda, and the people of our valley. And . . ." she tossed her head, unable to sort out the right words, "and give John the strength to deal with his feelings about Cassie Hytower. Amen."

## Chapter Nine

Luke was mired in a bog of infinite blackness. Weird dreams broke into the lengthy periods of sleep and unconsciousness, but the darkness was too thick and heavy for him to penetrate. Each time he tried to break the surface the tides and eddies pulled him back down into a pit of oblivion.

From somewhere outside, beyond the far reaches of his confines, he heard the murmurs of a soft whisper. At first he was sure it was an angel, beckoning him to let go of his worldly restraints. However, there was something familiar about the heavenly sound; it was a voice he had heard before. He strained within the boundaries of the black void, struggling to become cognizant. After a few agonizing moments, he was able to decipher the melodious words of encouragement.

"Come on, you big dummy!" the angel was badgering him. "Open your eyes and look at me, before I drag you out and dump you in the nearest watering trough!"

Luke sought the moisture to form words of his own. "Worst bedside manner I ever heard," he mumbled though his dry, cracked and swollen lips.

He was vaguely aware of a gasp of surprise. Then a damp cloth was pressed to his forehead. An instant later, a trickle of water entered his mouth to soothe his parched throat.

''About time you stopped playing possum. I knew you weren't hurt.'' Timony's words were stern, but Luke was incredibly warmed by the underlying tenderness he perceived. He used a measure of his limited strength to pry open the heavy-plated eyelids. It was no less work that picking up his horse with one hand.

The reward was worth the effort. His first glimpse within the room was of Timony leaning over him. She wore her hair loose and it cascaded about her shoulders. There was concern in her features, while her cerulean-colored eyes shown brightly.

''I was right,'' he said, working to rid his brain of the thick fog. ''I knew it was an angel.''

''Don't try using some worn line on me, Luke Mallory! I haven't forgiven you one bit. You broke my heart.''

''If I did, I deserve to be dragged another mile behind a horse.''

She didn't react to his words, but asked: ''Who did this to you?''

''Some fellers that I aim to visit again one day soon.''

''This isn't your fight.''

''Tell that to my aching body,'' he replied. ''Sure feels as if those boys were making this personal.''

''What were you doing on Black Diamond range?''

''Reckon I must have gotten lost.''

''Or you were sticking your nose into our fight!''

Luke blinked against the burning in his eyes. He didn't have a muscle or bone in his body that didn't hurt. ''My lips are sure feeling sore,'' he said. ''How about a little kiss to make them all better?''

Timony jerked back. "You never change!"

"I still have a big hankering for you, if that's what you mean."

"Yes, I've seen how much you care for me," she was angry once more. "No word, not even a letter for months on end. Then you come back to Broken Spoke without any warning, and do you come and see me? No!"

Luke was not strong enough to restrain Timony physically. When she backed up from the bed, he could only turn his head enough to follow her with his eyes.

"I'm right sorry," he said. "Reckon I didn't have the guts to admit to you that I was a failure."

"A failure!" she scathed. "Working for Wells Fargo was only a job! I was willing to be your wife! You put that stupid job ahead of me!" She was fully pumped up, full of vinegar and fire. "The next man I fall in love with will have to do a whole lot better than that, Luke Mallory. I'll never be second to anyone or anything else again. Do you hear me?"

"I hear, but . . ."

"You better heal up quick," she continued to scald him with her words. "Heal up and then get out of Broken Spoke. You don't have any reason to enter into this fight and get yourself killed."

"Timony, I . . ."

"And I told you, don't call me Timony! You don't have that right!"

Luke wondered what happened to the tenderness he had heard in her voice a few minutes earlier. As Timony whirled about and stormed from the room, he felt he would have been a whole lot better off had he remained unconscious. That little lady was about as unforgiving as a swatted hornet.

He heard the door slam, but it was opened again almost at once. Bunion came into the room, thoughtfully rubbing his beard. "From the way Timony left footprints up my chest and down my back on the way to her horse, I kind of figured you must have come around, Mallory."

"I think she's still a little miffed at me."

"Miffed? More like ready to scalp you with a dull knife."

"How long have I been out?"

"You didn't come around at all yesterday."

Luke tested his arms and legs. Everything seemed to work. "Guess I'm not hurt all that bad."

"I'm glad you're the one saying that, son. All the same, I don't think I'll pass over a mirror for you to take a gander at your reflection for a day or two. Wouldn't want you to have one of those relapses."

Luke lifted a hand and gingerly ran his fingers over his face. "Now that you mention it, I don't remember my head being so large and bumpy before."

"You got more knots than a forest of oak trees, that's the truth."

"What's going on in the valley? Is John still having his meeting?"

"Yeah, but I don't think you're up to attending yet."

"Tito gone?"

Bunion's head bobbed up and down. "And the Herefords are only thirty miles or so away. Twenty-five bulls." He sighed. "I'll bet that set old Hytower back a few coins."

"I heard of a single one selling for several thousand dollars some months back."

"The man is plum serious about building himself a herd."

Luke tested his strength, but he was in no condition to be out of bed yet. He relaxed and closed his eyes. Only rest would heal his battered body. No matter how badly he wanted to get up and around, he knew he had to stay put.

"I've got some mush and a loaf of fresh bread from the bakery. You need to eat something."

"Thanks, Bunion. I owe you."

"Don't worry about it," the old man quipped, "it'll all be on your bill."


The meeting had not yet been called to order before trouble arrived. Even as Cartwell was trying to take an informal role, the four Irish farmers came barging through the door of the Ace High saloon.

"We're closed for an hour or so, fellows," he told them.

"It isn't to be drinking that we've come," one of the men announced. "I'm Kevin McGreevy, and me friends and I are here to attend the meeting. 'Tis an oversight that we weren't invited, I'm sure."

John was the one who moved to confront the four men. He measured them to be as Bunion had once described, bindle stiffs, ex-miners, lean and hard as tempered steel. Facing off against Kevin, the two of them were about even in height and within a few pounds in weight.

"It wasn't an oversight, McGreevy. You weren't invited on purpose."

Kevin showed a mirthless smile. "Do you be knowing how that hurts our feelings, gov'nor? We could take offense at such an act."

"Take whatever you want," Billy spouted, moving

over to join John. "That's the way you Irish think anyway, taking what you want!"

"Is it slandering the Irish race you are?" Kevin challenged.

"Only four of its countrymen," John took up the gauntlet, "four hired squatters who are trying to take our land and water."

"We were invited to settle upon land which is free for the taking, Fairbourn," Kevin replied. "Mr. Hytower assured us that only a handful of lazy squatters and some greedy cattle owners were occupying this valley." He grinned. "That would be you."

"My family has been here for ten years, McGreevy. Von Gustin and Big George were here before me, and Fielding came with his sheep five years back. The farmers are hard-working men who moved here with a dream to own their own land, to have a family and live in peace. You're the squatters, not us."

Strangely enough, Kevin appeared to consider John's words. However, Dory and Chad Queen moved up beside John. Miller was close behind. He shouted: "I say we string up these four Irish dogs!"

There was a forward movement by a number of men in the room, but John held them back.

"Is that the way it is, Fairbourn?" Kevin asked. "It takes a whole room full of you blokes to take on four Irish?"

John gave Kevin a second appraisal. He recognized him as a fighting man, solid, keen of wit, who would be as hard to put down as a dust devil. He had a battle scar above one eye and a nose that had been broken at least once.

"No need to get a lot of people involved," he said

with a quiet authority. "If you need a lesson in how determined we are to keep what we have worked for, I'm your meat."

Kevin's eyes brightened, smiling without the use of his mouth. "Aye, gov'nor," he drawled, "it's you and me then."

The entire body of men followed the two men out to the street. Kevin took up a position in the middle of the crowd. He waiting and watched, while John pulled his buckskin gloves from his back pocket and put them on.

"Is it protecting your dainty pinkies you are?" he taunted him.

"A little something I learned from a Wells Fargo teamster once," John replied. "I gave him the beating, but my knuckles were still healing long after he had mended up good as new."

"Not to worry," Kevin showed a confident grin, "you'll not be hitting me enough to do any damage to your precious hands."

The men had formed a wide circle, with most calling for John to break Kevin's bones and grind him under his heel. The Irish were standing together, the three of them encouraging Kevin to be the victor.

John had always had keen reflexes and been quick with his hands. He had gone toe to toe with only three men in his life, but he knew how to fight. With a boxer's insight, he measured his opponent.

Kevin raised his fists out in front of his chest, not quite as high as John chose for his own guard. He sized up the Irishman as a brawler, a rough-and-tumble fighter who would rely on his strength and endurance to best his adversary. That gave him a degree of strategy.

As one, they came together. Two bulls butting heads

would have made less impact. Hard, vicious blows were exchanged, as each man sought a weakness in the other. Kevin was a whirlwind, launching a blur of punches at John. He made contact with a few, but John used his forearms to ward off a good many shots.

After the flurry, John countered, directing his attack with precision, jabbing for the man's nose, clubbing him about the head, then working on his body. As he carried forward the contest, he held a reserve, aware that the fight was not going to be settled with any one punch. His goal was to wear the man down a little at a time.

Five minutes of furious battle left both men winded, but there was no quit in either of them. Kevin gulped his second wind and came wading in, trying to get close.

John gave ground and used his jab, poking a fist into Kevin's face, keeping the man at bay. He dodged and weaved, struck with the sting and quickness of a bull-whip, then moved out of range. Kevin shook off the punishment and followed him doggedly, a relentless fighter, eager for the kill. As the fight progressed, he dismissed concern about keeping up his guard, trying only to inflict damage on John.

A jab rocked the Irishman's head back. Before he recovered, a set of leather-clad knuckles hit him flush in the jaw. It was hard enough that it backed him up a step. For the first time in the physical duel, a glimmer of apprehension entered Kevin's eyes. He shook off the hard jolt, but he was slowing down. Gasping for air, he searched for the reserve energy to continue.

John saw Kevin's mouth was open to draw in air. His chest was heaving from the intense exertion. The sting was still in his fists, but the power had slackened from his punches. Kevin was about spent.

Still using the bob and weave, John found his mark with a number of solid shots. He kept working him, conserving as much strength as possible. Panic seeped into Kevin's game. He began throwing wild, harmless swings that got mostly air.

John watched for his opening, slipped inside to pound away on the man, then backed off and waited again. The outcome of the competition was growing obvious. Kevin had a relentless tenacity, but very little strength left. He was growing weak, jaded from the extended effort. In a final attempt to win, he made a desperate charge at John, fists flying, using an all-out assault to try and turn the tide, to somehow get the upper hand.

John covered up, using his high guard to ward off blows to his head, ducking when he could, dodging a few shots, while allowing Kevin to burn his precious energy and waste potency with every punch. A set of knuckles caught him in the eye, another about took off an ear, and he had the warm, salty taste of blood in his mouth. Even so, he kept his feet under him, moving away, crouching and defending his head and body. When he sensed that Kevin was near exhaustion, he stopped the retreat and righted himself.

He exploded a mighty right hand against Kevin's jaw that stunned him to a dead stop. A sudden shock swept into the man's eyes. Kevin gave ground, with John on the offensive. The trauma of defeat sprang into the Irishman's face. His energy was spent. An uppercut lifted the man onto his heels, only to have a pile-driving right fist sink into his middle and double him over. Two more brutal shots sent him to his knees.

Kevin rocked there, dazed, bleeding, arms limp at his sides, panting for air. His head tipped to one side, as if its weight was too great for his neck to support. Positioned in such a way, sitting back on his heels, he still refused to go all the way down. In such a pose, John could have hammered him unmercifully. The shouts of some of the farmers and ranchers urged him to do just that. John backed off and lowered his fists.

"Finish him!" Miller cried. "You've got him!"

John threw a hard look at the man. "Fight's over!" he snarled the words. "It's done with!"

The Irish moved in to help Kevin, while John removed his gloves and walked over to the nearest watering trough. He tucked the gloves into his pocket and began to rinse the blood from his face.

"You took him good," Billy was there to help, offering him a bandanna to wet and hold against the swelling of his eye. "Had me worried for the first little bit, when you were letting him do all the hitting."

"He was too gall-durn sturdy to take on in a stand-up exchange. I had to wear him down."

"I've always said you were tougher than parched leather, big brother."

"You hear him before the fight?" John asked, ignoring the praise. "The Irish were told that we were no better than squatters."

"So?"

"I hope I proved that idea wrong."

Billy paused, looking past the crowd. "McGreevy and the others are leaving. Looks as if Kevin is moving under his own power." He gave a shake of his head. "Talk about a hard customer. You had him out cold, beat to within an inch of his life, and he gets up and walks away a minute later."

"There was no give in that man, Billy. I'm lucky to have been the last one standing."

"What now?"

"We continue our meeting. We have to remain organized."

# Chapter Ten

Cassie fearfully listened from the next room. Whenever Preston became angry, she had to walk as if on a bed of eggs. It took very little for him to turn his wrath on her.

"Nothing I could do to stop them," Preston was complaining.

"Who'd have thought those Irish dogs would lose their nerve?" Yarrow growled. "If I'd have been here, I'd have sent them crawling back to their holes!"

"It wouldn't have done any good to threaten them. They were determined to quit. I paid them off and they're gone."

"So what about their claims?"

"You said that you had a couple men coming in with the Hereford bulls?"

"Yeah, Button and Pincher. I've worked with both of them before."

"Then you need only find two more. We'll send them to Cheyenne and assume the claims of the Irish. We can still control the valley, but we must move quickly."

"What about the plan concerning the dam?"

"Everything goes as planned. Soon as you're ready we'll send the dynamite up to the canyon. Once the river is diverted, we'll have the rest of the worthless squatters in the valley by the throat."

"I'll touch base with Quanto and then pick up the herd. The bulls are just outside of town."

"Any news from Quanto on what's happening?"

"He said the meeting was mostly talk. John was not so full of fight, after tangling with McGreevy. The others threw around a few notions, like sending a petition to the territorial governor, that sort of thing. The only ones wanting a fight were the Queen boys. They wanted to load their guns and come spoiling for a showdown."

"That family had to have been hatched from spoiled eggs," Preston said. "I doubt they have ever had an actual intelligent thought between the three of them."

"I'm of the same mind, Preston. If the bunch of them dropped dead, vultures probably wouldn't touch their carcasses."

"I'll have Mont keep watch, in case they come snooping around. You best send Chico or Dawg to meet the bulls. Have the others keep up a patrol until the cattle arrive."

"All right. What about you?"

"I'm going to make a trip into town and send a wire to Governor Hoyt. He wants to remain in power for as long as possible. I shall remind him of my intention to financially support him. If the local peasants send him a petition, I need to know that it will end up buried or tossed out with the garbage."

"Good thinking."

Cassie sensed the conversation was about over. She quickly went into the bedroom and began to change the bedding, so Preston wouldn't know she had overheard them talking. There was a sense of relief in her that the men had come to a solution without Preston growing angry. He treated her well, except when things went wrong with his plans.

She tried to sort out what she had overheard. The Irish had quit, there had been a meeting by the farmers and ranchers, and Yarrow was concerned about a possible attack. Preston's idea of moving in and seizing control of the entire valley had hit a few snags.

Removing the expensive bed sheets, she paused to stare at the wall. She wished that things were different. It would not have been as hard being married to Preston, if he ever attempted to speak to her as a man to his wife. She was not a person, only a listening post, an ear for his problems. In their two years of marriage, he had never once asked how she felt about an issue. It was difficult to not be a real wife. Preston had chosen her, picked her out, as he would have a suit from a rack of clothes. The first year had been a tireless string of tutors, hired to train and educate her so that she would not be an embarrassment to him. She was a trophy, a prize which the man could dress up and show off at parties and social events, nothing more.

For a moment, Cassie thought back to the choice that put her at the man's beck and call. Her mother had been so very sick, their money gone, the landlord threatening to throw them out. There had seemed no other way.

She took a deep breath and swallowed the grief. If only her father hadn't died of a weak heart, if only her mother had not fallen ill, if only there had been friends and relatives to rally around, if only. . . .

Shaking the thoughts from her head, she was not the sort of person to dwell upon the adversities of her fate. She was here, this was now. Nothing could change what had happened.

However, there were other issues at hand, where she could sway the balance of power. If John knew how and when Preston was going to alter the course of the creek, he would be able to stop it. She had looked into his eyes and seen his strength, courage, honesty, and something else. For a moment, a warmth crept up her throat and into her cheeks. She had also recognized his desire. If she were to admit the truth, it was a mirror of her own.

*No!* she cursed the momentary frailty. She was a married woman! She couldn't feel that way about another man, she couldn't!

The vows held a hollow insincerity. Cassie tried to maintain a firm control on her emotions, but there was something about John, about the way he looked at and through her, as if he could freely explore the depths of her soul. The single touch of his hand had sent a shiver down her spine, a tingle of delight that stirred her very core of existence. As resolved as she tried to be, her heart was bent upon girlish daydreaming.

Forcing the ardent thoughts from her head, she worked on a plan that would aid the ranchers and farmers. It would only take a few words to Billy or John. If she could find a way to speak to one of them, Preston's precious plans would be derailed. Even as she heard Yarrow leave the house, she was thinking of alternatives.

"Tis a teller of falsehoods he was," Kevin spat the words, speaking to Luke and Bunion. "Squatters and lazy beggars he told us, worth no more nevermind than carpetbaggers."

Luke was sitting up on the bunk, still perplexed by the surprise visit. "So you men were hired to stake claims for Hytower. Then he was to buy the land from you, as soon as you had deeds?''

Kevin could only see out of one eye, so it was an odd gesture when he winked with the other. ''Aye, that was the plan.''

''And now you've up and quit, the lot of you?''

''I know when a man is fighting to save face and when he's fighting for his family and honor. We'll not be a part of what Mr. Hytower has in mind.''

''I apologize for what I've thought of you men,'' Luke said seriously. ''My impression was that you were convicts, paid bullies for Hytower.''

Kevin waved off the admission. ''If the truth be told, Mr. Mallory, at the time we were hired, our place of residence *was* behind bars. T'was involved in a coal mining dispute we were, and Hytower paid our fines and offered us employment.''

''Now what?''

He grinned. ''We're more of a mind to return to digging for ore than wet-nursing a piece of dusty, rock-hard land. Our claims will be turned back, the conditions of settlement unfulfilled.''

An idea crept forth in Luke's head. ''May I make a suggestion?''

Timony was churning butter when she heard the wagon roll into the yard. Grateful for the chance to give her arms a rest, she walked over and looked out the window. It came as a surprise to see the visitor was none other than Cassie Hytower and her uncle Mont. With a curious fascination, Timony opened the door and stepped out onto the porch.

''Hello, Miss Fairbourn,'' Cassie was the one to

speak. From the way her eyes darted quickly about, Timony knew she had been hoping to speak to someone else. It didn't take any real pondering to know who.

"Mrs. Hytower," she replied evenly. "Nice of you to stop by."

Cassie was immediately serious. "I wonder if you would get word to your brother, John. I know he is the head of the Ranchers' Association."

"Of course."

"Ask him if he can be at the Sunday meeting tomorrow. I need to speak to him in private—only for a moment!" she hurried to add.

Timony raised an eyebrow, perplexed about Mont Hytower sitting there, seemingly oblivious to their conversation. He stared off into space, as if enjoying the pleasant breeze and the warm spring sun. It occurred to her that John had told her correctly; Mont was not all that fond of his nephew.

"I'll tell him," Timony finally replied. "I'm sure he'll find time to be at the meeting."

"He is all right, isn't he?" She seemed uncomfortable at the way that sounded. "I mean, I heard about him fighting with one of the Irishmen."

"John won the fight," she told her. "My brother isn't moved to violence very often, but when he is, he usually wins." She furrowed her brow in sincerity. "You can tell that to your husband."

Cassie might have taken offense, but she appeared to dismiss the barb. "If you would pass along my request, I'd be most grateful."

"I'll tell him."

Cassie turned to Mont. "Let's go, uncle."

The old gentleman struck up the team and drove the

wagon from the yard. Even before they were out of sight, Linda came from the foreman's house. She had been watching and seemed to be as puzzled by the visit as Timony.

"Was that who I think it was?"

"Stopped by with a message for John."

The disapproval shone at once in Linda's face. "She's a married woman. She shouldn't be chasing after your brother."

"John thinks she has a conscience about what Preston is doing."

"A woman is supposed to stick by her man, not go taking sides against him. I don't care what he is or does, she married him." With her chin raised she added, "A woman makes the bed she sleeps in."

"I'm not taking her side, Linda, but John thinks Cassie might have been forced to marry Preston."

"When you're a wife, you're a wife," she argued. "You take the good with the bad, and you stick it out."

"There's a rumor that Preston beats her."

Linda had been sitting tall in the saddle, but that news loosened her cinch. "Who told you that?"

"Cole told John. I guess Tito interrupted one of Preston's temper tantrums when he delivered his load of supplies."

"I never held with that sort of thing," Linda said. "There isn't any reason why a woman should have to put up with being abused." Then with a returned haughtiness, "But it still don't excuse her chasing after your brother."

"No, it doesn't."

"You going to tell John about the visit?"

"Yes. I'm sure it must be important."

"Well, suit yourself. Me, I'd keep quiet. I'm not about to help someone commit a sin."

Timony bit back the harsh words that rose to surface. With a steady voice, she said: "John has not committed a sin, Linda. He feels sorry for the lady. I can understand that."

"As long as his sympathy has its limitations. It ain't a wide margin between crying on a man's shoulder to kissing him on the mouth!"

"You know John is not going to do that."

"Even Samson had his weakness for a woman."

Timony let the argument end on that note. "Want me to help you fix something to eat? I have to ride into town after lunch."

"I put together a venison stew last night. I was going to warm up the leftovers."

"Sounds good."

Linda took a step, then rotated back around to peer at Timony. "I could make up a bowl, so's you could take it with you."

"Whatever for?"

"Am I stupid?" she asked bluntly. "To take to the Wells Fargo gent. As you haven't been spending all of your time in town, I have to assume he's on the mend."

"You think you're pretty smart, don't you?"

"It don't take any brains to know you've been miserable the past few weeks. Why don't you go in and make up with him? He was a louse, but he's sorry. You want to punish him until he gives up and leaves Broken Spoke?"

"No."

''Come on, Timony. We can talk while I heat up the stew.''

''I'll get the butter churn. I have to finish with it before I leave.''

## Chapter Eleven

Quanto made his report while Yarrow listened in silence. When he had finished, Yarrow sent him off to get some rest and went in to inform Hytower.

"So, what's going on?" Preston asked, before he'd even had time to remove his hat.

"It don't make any sense, Mr. Hytower. Quanto says the Fairbourns are out checking their new calves, the Cline family is farming as usual, even the Queen boys are tending to business."

"What about the meeting? You told me they had made some plans."

"Seems as if it was nothing but talk. It appears that they're taking a wait-and-see approach to all of this."

"Even after the boys roughed up Mallory?"

"Should have picked us a farmer or one of the locals, I guess. Your orders were to grab the first one we could and make an example of them. Doesn't look as if it did us any good."

"Perhaps you're mistaken on that point, Yarrow," Preston said, displaying an air of confidence. "It could be why there is no reprisal. Perhaps it is why the people are sitting back and doing nothing. They are afraid to butt heads with us."

"I understand the action. You wanted to send a message."

"So what is wrong with that?"

"I'm a firm believer in throwing the first punch or firing the first shot, but I think we should have picked a real target—maybe John Fairbourn."

"Kevin McGreevy didn't have much success with him."

"Dawg and the boys were not bound by any rules of fair play. Kevin picked himself the toughest bronc in the corral to ride." He uttered a grunt of disgust. "I still can't believe those four all packed their gear and ran."

"Soon as the bulls are turned to pasture, I want to settle the claims in Cheyenne."

"The herd is only a couple miles down the road. They will be in the holding pasture before dark. We should be able to leave first thing in the morning."

"Good. It's imperative we keep title to the land on either side of the gap."

"I understand," Yarrow said. "Soon as we get some new names on those claims, we can go to work on the creek."

"Correct. We need those claims to keep within any legal boundaries. If trouble comes, then we'll do what has to be done."

The two stopped their conversation, as Mont and Cassie entered the yard. The team stopped long enough for Cassie to get down. She removed a burlap sack from the boot, then Mont drove the carriage over to put up the horses.

"Your shopping didn't take long," Preston said, eyeing the small bundle. "Must not have needed very much."

"I was hoping there would be some fresh vegetables,

but I suppose it's too early in the season. I did buy some lemons, so we could have lemonade.''

"Nothing else?"

"Your pipe tobacco arrived."

Preston cheered up at the news. "That's good. I was down to the dregs of my last pouch.''

Yarrow came out to stand next to him. Cassie immediately averted her gaze. She hated the way he looked at her, always vile and dirty. She sometimes wondered how Preston could be so blind as to not notice.

"See any of those Irish dogs in town?"

"The lady at the store said they didn't stay more than a few minutes. When the Saturday stage left, they were on board.''

"Any other gossip?"

Cassie glanced at Preston. She hated Yarrow's impertinence. What kind of husband allowed the hired help to grill his wife about every detail of her shopping trip? With a short sigh, she said, "No, nothing."

"How about the Wells Fargo man?"

"You mean the one your hired bullies about killed?"

"He was trespassing."

"I'm sure he was."

"Cassandra!" Preston reacted at once to the ire in her voice, "Did you hear anything about him or not?"

"I didn't ask, and the lady didn't offer any information on him. As I am married to the man who ordered his beating, I hardly think she would bring up the subject.''

"Don't you be sassing me," he warned.

Cassie was immediately repentant. "I didn't mean for it to sound that way, Preston. Really!"

"Seems as if she sometimes forgets who's side she's

on,'' Yarrow was there to instantly dig in his spurs. ''I think she's taken a liking to Fairbourn.''

Only anger helped Cassie to hide the truth of Yarrow's words. ''You're a disgusting human being!''

Yarrow and Preston both laughed at her indignation. It offered Cassie the chance at an exit, and she took it, retreating quickly into the house.

Timony was crestfallen. ''Gone?'' she murmured. ''Mr. Mallory is gone?''

Cole leaned on his cane, while his head bobbed up and down. ''Warn't an hour after the stage this morning. Didn't even say good-bye to Harlot. She's been moping around all day, like she done lost her best friend.''

Timony's mood was not lightened by his attempt at humor. ''He didn't leave a letter or something?''

''Sorry, missy,'' Cole said softly. ''He didn't say a word to anyone. Bunion provided him a horse and tack, then he up and road out of Broken Spoke.''

''I can't believe he would run from the likes of Yarrow's men.''

''Maybe he didn't think he had a reason to fight. The two of you done broke harness, didn't you?''

She squirmed. ''I don't know. He might have taken it that way.''

''Taken what?''

''My telling him to get out of town, that this wasn't his fight.''

Cole scratched his head. ''Can't see how a man could take that wrong.''

''I didn't mean it!'' she cried. ''He knew I didn't mean it!''

''You sure about that?''

Timony felt the weight of the world, crushing the very life out of her. "No," she said weakly, "no, I'm not."

"Want to send a wire? We might catch him at Cheyenne."

"Why Cheyenne?"

"I don't rightly know. Maybe he said something about going there."

"You said he left without a word."

Cole's face revealed that he hadn't told her all he knew. Timony reached over and grabbed his cane. With a jerk, she pulled it away from him.

"Hey!"

"You tell me what you know, Mr. Cole, or I'm going to use this on you."

"He didn't tell me nothing, Timony! For pity's sake! Don't be messing with my walking stick!"

"Why Cheyenne?" she demanded.

"I don't know. Bunion said he thought Mallory was going to Cheyenne. You'd have to ask him why."

"You're holding out on me, Jack Cole. You better tell me, before I take Harlot out and use her for coyote bait!"

"All I know is what Bunion told me. He seemed to have some idea of what Mallory was going to do."

Timony shoved the cane back into his hand. "I'll talk to him."

"Yeah, sure," Cole grunted the words. "Me you threaten, him you'll talk to."

Bunion must have seen her coming. When Timony arrived, he was inside the corral fence, peeking between the boards like a mischievous child playing hide and seek.

"Come out and face me like a man, Bunion!" she snapped.

"Not so long as you've got your hackles raised," he said. "I'd never be able to show my face again, if'n I was to take a whupping from a woman."

"Coward!"

"Calling me names won't do you no good. I'm staying right here."

Timony gave thought to climbing over the fence, but decided against it. "Tell me what you know about Mallory. Why did he go to Cheyenne and is he coming back?"

"I thought you told him that you never wanted to see him again."

"I said no such thing."

"Didn't you tell him to get out of Broken Spoke?"

"It's none of your business what I told him. What did he tell you?"

"Simmer down, young lady."

"Start talking, Bunion, or I'll climb over that fence and pull your beard out—one hair at a time!"

Bunion puckered up and wrinkled his nose. "Boy, howdy! I never knew you to have such a temper before. All these years, I been telling people how level-headed you were, how you was always pleasant to be around and in control of your emotions. This ain't like you, Timony."

She took hold of the fence and found a foothold. "Whoa!" he cried, before she started to climb. "I'll tell you what I know!"

"So talk!"

"Mallory said he was going to Cheyenne, I think maybe to see about getting his old job back, becoming a teamster for Wells Fargo again."

"What about coming back here?"

"He said he'd be back, but he didn't say when."

Timony took a deep breath and let it out slowly. There it was, the same as before. She was supposed to sit and wait, pace the floor for endless days and nights. How could Luke be so cold and callous? Didn't he have any consideration for her at all? Tears stung the back of her eyes, threatening to flood down her cheeks. She let go of the fence and quickly turned her back to Bunion, so he wouldn't see her crying.

"Thank you," she managed, withholding the sob that rose into her throat.

"You know he's coming back, Timony," Bunion's words were suddenly soft, filled with concern. "He'd be the biggest fool in Wyoming territory not to come for you."

She swallowed hard, but knew her voice would crack if she tried to speak again. With a shrug of her shoulders, she walked away from the livery. Never would she have thought that there could be so much pain involved in loving a man.

As was his habit, after their trip from the Sunday meeting in town, Mont stopped the carriage, so Cassie could get out at the front of the house, then he drove the team over to the barn. Cassie opened the door to find Preston and Yarrow waiting. A dread apprehension flooded through her, as she looked into Preston's face.

"Ask her what she was talking about," Yarrow sneered the words. "She done sat right on Fairbourn's lap. I seen it all."

Cassie's heart began to pound fearfully. She would have bolted and ran, but there was no place to which she could make an escape.

"Well?" Preston demanded. "What were you doing, Cassandra? What did you tell John Fairbourn?"

"I-I didn't . . ."

Preston sprang forward and grabbed her arms. With a vicious twist, he threw her against the wall. Cassie bounced off the hardwood partition and fell to her hands and knees. Before she could get her brain to function, he had a handful of her hair, yanking her up onto her feet.

"You dirty little traitor!" he screamed, totally out of control. "You've been seeing that man behind my back! You no-good, cheating tramp!"

"Ought to take a whip to her," Yarrow encouraged him. "Bet she's told him our every move."

"Is that right?" Preston yelled the words. "How long has this been going on?"

"No! It isn't true!" Cassie cried. "I only asked about Mr. Mallory."

"Sure you did," Yarrow was the one to scoff at her explanation. "As if you had any reason to care what happened to that ex-Wells Fargo teamster."

"I haven't forgotten that Yarrow caught you two together at the house. Quanto says you and Mont rode over to the Fairbourn place yesterday too." He slapped her hard across the face! "What kind of game are you playing, Cassandra?" he snarled vehemently. "Whose side are you on?"

Cassie was stung by the smarting blow. Tears came into her eyes. She was terrified of Preston when he was riled. Once his temper took over, he had no sense. The apology after a beating never stopped the pain and suffering he inflicted. She was humiliated at being confronted, and trapped by the actual circumstances. To be silent was to let Preston think the worst.

"I haven't cheated on you, Preston," she whimpered the words. "You know I wouldn't do that."

"She's lying!" Yarrow continued to provoke Preston's anger. "I seen the way they looked at each other the day he come to the ranch. Sure as we're standing here, she's sold us out!"

Preston drew back his fist. Cassie closed her eyes tightly and ducked her head, expecting to feel the shock and pain of the brutal contact. But the door opened to save her.

"What's going on?" It was Mont. "Nephew, have you lost your mind?"

Preston pointed a finger at his uncle. "You've been helping her behind my back, you deceitful, worthless old man. The two of you are out to ruin my empire!"

Mont put his hands on his hips and glared at Preston. "What a prize fool my brother raised for a son! I've known that you were an animal all these years. I'll bet you have venom running through your veins instead of blood." He was red in the face with ire. "I'm not going to stand here and let you beat Cassie again."

"The only thing you're going to do is get out of here, old man," Yarrow told him. "You've been working hand-in-hand with this back-stabbing witch."

"All either of us want is to stop Preston from doing like his old man and hurting innocent people," Mont replied boldly. "Garth was a vile, uncaring monster. He worked the people in his plant like the lowest kind of slaves and under inhuman conditions. No heat in the winter, a blast furnace in the summer, the poor wretches had to stand for twelve hours a day over machines until

130 Terrell L. Bowers

their fingers were bleeding and raw. Then, when they became sick or injured and could no longer work, he would fire them.

"You're the spawn of that devil, Preston. You've no conscience, no moral fiber at all. You can only think of power, of owning more than anyone else, of becoming some kind of tin-plated god. You're nothing more than a sick and corrupt petty tyrant."

Preston was at the boiling point. "I want you off of my ranch, Mont. I've been carrying you like excess baggage all these months. Get out of here! Leave my ranch while you still can!"

"Do one thing right in your life, Preston," Mont replied. "Let me take Cassie away from here. She deserves a life."

"She deserves nothing but contempt!" Preston shot back. "I offer her the world, and she sneaks around behind my back to be with another man! I'd trade her to a pack of nomad Indians before I would let her go with you!"

Mont looked at Cassie. She could see the pain in his face, but there was nothing that either of them could do. He was too old to physically challenge Yarrow and Preston.

"I'll leave your ranch," Mont finally spoke, "but I'm staying in Broken Spoke. I'm going to see to it that you fail this time, Preston. I'm going to watch you get the beating that you've needed all of your selfish, miserable life!"

"If you stay in the valley, uncle, it'll be under six feet of earth. Yarrow, get him out of my sight!"

Yarrow took hold of Mont's shirt and dragged him out the front door. Cassie might have worried that he would hurt the elderly man, but she had no time to concern herself about him. Preston pulled her around and shoved her roughly back against the wall again.

"You vile little tramp!" he shouted. "When I think of all I've done for you, and this is how you thank me! I planned to build you the finest house for a thousand miles around, fill it with servants and all of the luxuries money can buy. I've spent a fortune to make you happy!"

She stared at him in awe. "Make me happy?" In spite of the seriousness of the situation, Cassie began to laugh. "You're such a hypocrite, Preston. The way you idolize yourself, there isn't room in your life for another love. You care nothing about anyone but yourself!"

"I took you away from poverty, out of a cardboard shack you called home. You were a dirty, ragged little doll, and I dressed you in the finest silks and made you a queen!"

"You extorted me into marrying you to save my mother's life. She had to be placed into a hospital or die from pneumonia." No longer holding back, she put acid into her words. "And she died all the same!"

"I held up my end of the bargain."

"Yes, but whose order was it to put her into the cold and damp cleaning room? Who kept her standing in icy water for hours on end, washing your rotten equipment? Who told her she would lose her job if she didn't show up for work, even though she was too sick to stand up?"

The truth shone within Preston's expression. Until that moment, Cassie had only suspected that the creature in front of her had manipulated the circumstances to force her into marriage. She could see it now, the guilt unconcealed in his face. Long before he negotiated a contract between them, he had put a plan into operation which had caused the death of her mother.

"You're a despicable, contemptible swine! And you have the gall to stand there and accuse me of betraying you!" She doubled her petite fists and glared at him. "If I were a man, I would stick you in an icy pit, make you stand for hours in cold water, let you work until your fingers were bleeding and numb, force you to endure the very treatment you inflicted upon so many of your workers! Then, when you were struck down with a cough that raked your insides, unable to catch your breath for wheezing and choking, suffering a fever that blurred your vision and set fire to your brain, then I would force you to continue at the job until you died on the spot!"

Preston's face worked, but he immediately calmed his emotions. There before her was the disciplined side of a cold-hearted despot. He accepted no blame for any action. It was not in his character.

"I can see that I made a mistake in picking you for my wife." The words were casual and emotionless, as if he were speaking of the weather. "Yarrow has made me an offer concerning you, Cassandra. I believe his idea has some merit."

"What?" she was aghast. "Yarrow?"

Preston turned his back to her. "Good-bye, young lady. I'm through with you."

She stood there, perplexed, staring in bewilderment at the man. Before she could summon any words to question him further, he marched smartly out of the house.

A panic rose within her at once. Yarrow had made an offer? What kind of offer was he talking about?

The sound of a wagon moving out in the yard caused her to run to the window. Mont was leaving the ranch.

Chico was sitting at his side, obviously there to make certain he went all the way to Broken Spoke, then to return with the wagon. Her only ally on the ranch was gone.

The door opened a moment later, while Cassie was still trying to get her brain to sort out what was going on. Yarrow was there, a cruel smile on his thin lips.

"Well, is this a fine turn of events or what, Cassandra?" he sneered in a mocking tone of voice. "It's you and me from now on."

"What do you mean by that?"

He waved a hand. "Oh, don't be so coy. You know what I'm talking about—you and me, me and you, the two of us, together."

"You're not serious! Preston and I are legally married!"

Yarrow lifted his shoulders in a careless shrug. "He's rich and powerful. Nobody is going to question him. When a man leaves a woman, it's desertion. When a woman leaves a wealthy tycoon like Preston, it's stupidity and a quick divorce. He'll have a thousand women throwing themselves at his feet within a month's time."

"But . . ." she couldn't get the words out.

"Once you're free of your wifely obligations with Preston, I'll be right there to take care of you." She opened her mouth to object, but he stopped her. "No need to thank me, my beauty. There will be plenty of time for you for you to show your gratitude."

"I'm not a horse to be traded, Yarrow."

His lips curled upward, "And I'm not one of those pinky-extended, milksops—like your ex-husband." There was frost in his eyes and his words were chilled with ice. "You're going to learn to serve me proper,

Cassie, or I'll run you through cactus barefoot and peel your hide with a skinning knife.''

Cassie sucked in her breath, a knot of terror churning within her chest. ''You can't get away with this. I'll . . .''

He grabbed her by the wrist and yanked her over to stand close to him. ''Don't tell me what I can and can't do, honey!'' He hissed every word, twisting her arm up behind her back. ''You're going to be mine now, so you best do as I tell you.'' He forced her arm upward until she cried out from the pain. ''You hear me?''

''Yes,'' she gasped. ''I hear you.''

He let go and gave her a push toward the bedroom. ''Get a few things together, just what you need. You're going to stay at the line shack until Preston confirms the divorce. Once you're no longer his wife, we'll get our own house. You'll serve me like a faithful wife, or else I'll give you to Quanto to trade to some of his Indian friends.''

Cassie backed away, then hurried into the bedroom. She was still in shock, but self-preservation kept her moving. As she threw items into a trunk, her mind was turning over possibilities. Preston was going to set her free of her marriage vows. Divorce was shameful for a woman, but anything was preferable to being Preston's wife, even living in disgrace.

Yarrow was the real problem. He wanted her for his personal slave, but she would never submit to him. Somehow, she was going to escape. It was only ten miles to Rocking Chair ranch. If she could reach John Fairbourn, she would be free, really free!

## Chapter Twelve

Tito listened to the idea, then frowned, thoughtfully. "It would be about as risky as kissing a rattlesnake on the lips, but it could work."

"So, will you help?"

"I don't know, Mallory. I've got my job to think about."

"It's only until you can get one of your cousins to help out. After six months, you won't be tied to anything."

"You ought to go into politics. You have a great way of skirting the real issue of the matter."

"And that is?"

"Don't con me, Mallory. You need a warm body for this scheme of yours, but mostly you want my gun on your side again."

"Can you blame me? I'm facing long odds, even with the other ranchers and farmers throwing in to help."

"Yarrow struck me as a dangerous man. He won't scare. You start this, it'll mean blood soaking the ground—could be your own."

"I know the chance I'm taking, but it's something I'm going to do."

Tito chuckled. "Yeah, I figured as much."

"I'd like your help, but it won't change my mind either way."

"You doing this for the glory of the fight, or for your gal?"

"I'm not concerned with any glory. I aim to do this because it's right."

He gave an exaggerated sigh. "Let me tell the boss to leave me off the schedule for a couple weeks. I'll ride with you."

Luke felt a fondness in his heart for the man. "You're a good friend, Tito."

"You can put that on my headstone: *Here lies Tito Pacheco, not real smart, but he was a friend.* Makes me feel so much better about getting killed."

Luke watched him walk over to the Wells Fargo office. He wished he had other options, rather than to get Tito involved, but who else could match Yarrow's gun? It would haunt him forever, if he got his friend killed, but Preston had to be stopped. To have a chance against Yarrow and his men, Luke needed someone like Tito to even the odds. Even recruiting him, it was likely that there would be a bloody war before this thing was over.

For a moment, he reflected on his life, the path he was taking, and considered the possible consequences. For five long years, he had worked diligently toward a solitary goal, to become a Wells Fargo agent. Until he met Timony, it had been the only thing in the world he wanted. Finally, when his objective was attained, he discovered that he was not cut out to be an agent. He didn't have either the daily patience required for a thousand transactions, nor the obsequious tact required when dealing with the pillars of society. He had grown to hate the long hours, the endless chores and the socializing for the benefit of the company. It was not his nature to rub elbows with the snobs of society, while sacrificing his freedom for the sake of an occupation. Even so, failure was a sour bite to swallow. He had become despondent and turned to drinking for the first time in his life. Nothing so wasted a man's brain and body as drowning his misery in hard drink. It was a road to certain destruction.

Remembering that it was Tito who forced him to turn from the bottle, he again hoped that his actions didn't bring the man's life to a tragic end. The plan was simple, but there would be repercussions. Hytower had invested a great deal of time, energy and money into his scheme. He would not give up his vision of an empire without a fight.

"You ready to ride?" Tito had returned without him being aware of it.

"Last chance to walk away, Tito. I can still do this alone."

He waved a hand to dismiss his concern. "You'd be dead before the end of the week, Mallory," he said grinning, "and you don't look all that good yet from your last go-round with Hytower's men. Besides, I was in need of some time off. This beats the fishing trip I had in mind."

"Yeah, but you would have been the one doing the catching. The fish I'm up against are going to want to use you as bait."

"If you're going to get all sentimental, I'll round up one of the local fiddlers to play us a sad tune."

Luke chuckled. "You're right. I sometimes forget that action used to be what you lived for."

"Be like old times."

The two men went for their horses. Each respected the other, and both knew their actions might have fatal results. It was a bond that spoke more than words.

*   *   *

Jack Cole was in the back of the room, pretending to be deeply involved in his solitaire game. He was along in years, but his hearing was still keen. Cartwell and Preston were in earnest conversation.

"I can't believe it," Cart was saying. "I saw your uncle Mont in town. I was surprised that he had rented a room above the general store."

"He stole some money from me, Mr. Devine. I take him in like my own father and he up and steals money right out of my house."

"You want me to call Cole over here to arrest him?"

"I don't wish a scandal, nor do I wish to see him imprisoned."

"Then what?"

"I would prefer that he takes one of the next stages out of town." He shoved a wad of money into Cart's hand. "This should pay for his ticket back east, back to wherever he wants to go. All I want is to put this behind me."

"I'll see what I can do."

"There is one other thing." Preston took a deep breath, as if it pained him to speak. "Cassandra ran away with one of the men who brought in the Hereford bulls. I can never forgive her for such an infidelity."

"Ran away?" Cart raised his brows in surprise.

"I wish to file for a divorce, effective at once."

"Well, I don't know about that, Preston. It's awfully tough to get a divorce decree. I'll have to wire for the petition papers, see about the legalities. . . ."

"You may wire the governor if you wish. I'm certain he will certify my rights. I'll pay whatever it costs. I want this episode ended, and I want it taken care of right away.''

''I'll send the wire first thing. If we can get a sanctioned judge to sign the papers, I don't see anything to stop the divorce.''

''How long will it take?''

''At least a few days. I don't really know.''

''Make it by the end of the week,'' Preston said haughtily. ''I don't wish to have this hanging over my head forever.''

''How about this cowboy? You want anything done about his stealing your wife?''

Preston uttered a cruel laugh. ''He'll suffer enough, once he's had her around for a while.''

Cart responded with a chuckle of his own.

A quick handshake and Preston was out of the room. Cart waited until he had his carriage headed out of town, before he walked over to Cole.

''You hear any of that?''

''Every word. Smells like week-old fish to me.''

''I don't like it one bit, Cole. A divorce and the old man kicked off of Black Diamond. It's like someone opened the floodgates. Everything is coming to a head at once.''

''You going to send off the wire?''

''Durn tootin'! It's the best thing that could happen for that little lady. If we get her a proper divorce, she might have a chance at a real life.''

''Society don't look with no favor on a divorcée,'' Cole said. ''But in this case, I got to agree with you that she'll be better off.''

Cart began to scribble on a piece of paper. ''This here ought to start things moving in the right direction.'' He paused. "Soon as you send off the wires, maybe you ought to pass the word to Bunion. He could make the ride up to the Rocking Chair and mention what is going on to John or one of the other Fairbourns. They ought to be kept abreast of these newest developments."

Cole was already thinking on those lines. "I'll do that."

## Chapter Thirteen

It had been four days and the house seemed hollow, empty without Cassandra to answer Preston's every command. Preston sat in the easy chair, sipped at the hard liquor and stared off into space. He wondered how Yarrow would treat his ex-wife. It was certain the little backstabbing witch was already regretting her decision to take sides against him. For a few minutes, he suffered with an aloneness, a depressive mood that darkened his world. Thinking back, he compared the disposition with a time when he had looked to his father for comfort.

His mother had suffered apoplexy and remained in bed for a full year, before finally succumbing. Garth had shown no emotion during the entire affair. Hired servants had cared for her, while maids continued to do all of the chores around the house. There had been no change in their daily existence, other than for one less person at the dinner table. At her funeral, Garth had been stolid, his façade never changing. He was of an iron will, a man who appreciated and accepted no less than complete success. Garth considered the showing of tears or compassion as a display of weakness. Preston had learned to be strong, even ruthless. It was the only way to win praise from his father.

Tipping the glass, he emptied the last of the drink. He

wondered why he was not satisfied with his life. Following in his father's footsteps, to be king would not have been enough. The man had taken a meager stake and created a thriving business. He had made a fortune, bought the finest house and furniture that money could buy. The governor called him for advice, senators and congressmen invited him to their fund-raisers, a hospital had named a research building after him. He had built an empire from a handful of dust. Preston would settle for nothing less.

With a shrug, he dismissed the melancholy sensations. After the ranch was thriving, he would find himself a proper queen to sit next to his throne. There were dozens, hundreds, of women who would flock to throw themselves at his feet. He would be more selective the second time around. He would choose a mate like a fine wine, taste the many vintages available, assure himself that the one he favored was mature, yet with a delicate touch and a sensitive demeanor. He would offer her a life of luxury and social prominence, and she would be willing to serve his every need.

His first order of business was to hire a housekeeper. He might take his pick of those available in the valley, or he could import a specially trained servant from back east. Money and power were the only real things of value. When things were organized, he would build his house, acquire a cook, a maid, and possibly a groom for his horse and carriage too. He would soon become the king of all of Wyoming, as great a cattle baron as any in Texas. Once his herd arrived to cover the land, he would have the largest spread within a thousand miles. It cheered him to think that even his father would have been impressed by the grandeur and scope of his empire.

Yarrow abruptly opened the door without knocking. Preston decided he would have to change that habit, once all of the wrinkles were smoothed out of his plan. At the moment, he was concerned only with the frown on his foreman's face.

"I expected you back last night."

Yarrow hesitated. "I got in too late to talk to you." He waved a hand in the air. "Besides, what I found out would have kept you awake all night."

"Why? What's wrong?"

"We got to Cheyenne about a day late."

"What are you talking about?"

The red tint to Yarrow's face told of his vexation. "The only good news I have is that your divorce has been awarded." He handed him a brown envelope. "Cartwell says everything is legal. You're a single man again."

Preston tossed the envelope onto a chair. "What about Cheyenne?"

"The boys came back empty-handed. Someone has already assumed the claims of the Irish."

"What?"

"That's right. The titles had already been transferred on all four homesteads. We no longer own the property that controls the flow of Dakota Creek."

"But who—?"

"Mallory."

Preston swore vehemently. "The meddling fool! We should have acted sooner."

"One day didn't seem very long at the time. Question is, now what?" Yarrow asked. "If we don't have the water, we can't gain control of the valley. It'll mean waging war against every farmer and cattleman in Broken Spoke. We hadn't intended on a fight like that.''

"Get Dawg and the others. Send them to do the job on the river, before Mallory and his friends know what's happening. According to those engineers, once we collapse the walls of the gorge and turn the creek, it will be next to impossible for them to reroute it back.''

"We won't be on legal ground this time. They have claim to the land where the river comes through the gap.''

"The only law out here is gun law! The new course of the Dakota will put it under our control. I still hold the claim to over a thousand acres. We'll turn the creek toward the endless wasteland to the north. Every existing farm and ranch will dry up and blow away. The only one we'll have to fight for over the water will be the Fairbourns'.'' His face clouded. "And I look forward to that.''

"I'll get the boys rounded up," Yarrow said. "I'll send Dawg, Chico and the two new men. I think there's at least one other I can get too. Quanto is up at the line shack, keeping an eye on the Herefords. With him and me still here, the place won't be left undefended.

"The traitorous Irishers!" Preston raved wildly. "They did this to us.''

"Who would have thought a bunch of convicts would have any honor or a conscience?''

"You only have five or six men you can trust. Will that be enough?''

"I don't know, Preston. We thought Mallory was out of the picture. If he brought friends with him, we could be in for a real fracas.''

"Whatever it takes, Yarrow, however much it costs.''

But Yarrow was growing cautious. "We'll take the fight to them and see what happens. I've told you from the first that we would need more men if this came to a range war. If I had twenty men drawing gun wages, we would wipe out every farm and ranch in Broken Spoke."

"We can still go out and hire them! I need that creek to survive!"

Yarrow didn't reply, but spun about and hurried from the house. Preston followed him to the doorway and watched him mount up. The horse kicked up dust from its heels, as it left the yard at a gallop.

He didn't like the last look on Yarrow's face. He knew the man was not a coward, but he seemed reluctant to follow orders. How hard could it be to whip a bunch of hick farmers and saddle bums? Yarrow had talked the big man. Well, here was his chance to prove his worth and earn the high salary he paid the man.

*High salary?* he thought cynically, *I gave the swine my own wife! For that price, he ought to lay down his life for me a dozen times over!*

The thought of Cassandra nagged at him again. He had maneuvered her into marrying him, used every dirty trick he knew to win her hand. Why he hadn't been able to make her love him was a total mystery. He adorned her with the finest clothes, hired the best tutors, taught her to act and sound like a properly educated woman of society. He was rich, powerful, equal to most men in looks—what more did a woman want?

*Well, she's going to wish she had clung to my leg and kissed my feet!* he thought bitterly. Yarrow was not going to surround her with finery and maids. He would break her like a wild mare to a saddle, then he would crush her spirit and fire. He would mold her into a whimpering pup, eager to snap to his every command.

Preston set his teeth hard. ''Cassandra, you little fool! Why didn't you love me? How could you betray me for someone like John Fairbourn?''

Timony saw Bunion ride into the yard. She had been helping Linda with the laundry, but stopped to see what he wanted.

''Where is John?'' he asked, as soon as she appeared.

''He and Billy were going up to the north pasture first thing, then over and meet with Cline. We are considering stringing wire to keep Hytower's herd of cattle from grazing us out.''

''I need to get word to them right away, Timony. There's going to be more fireworks than on the Fourth of July.''

''What's going on?''

''Preston ordered his uncle off of his place and has divorced his wife.''

''That's not possible! It takes months, even years, to get a divorce!''

''Not with enough money behind you.''

Timony's heart began to pound. If Cassie was a free woman, John could. . . .

''But that isn't why I made the ride out,'' Bunion interrupted her thoughts. ''Mallory is going to need some help.''

''Mallory?''

''He and Tito, plus Tito's two cousins—the ones who work for Fielding—took over the claims of those four Irish farmers. They now control the flow of Dakota Creek.''

Timony was dumbfounded. "What?"

"They are expecting trouble, and it will only be Tito and Mallory against all of the guns Yarrow can send against them. The massive herd for Hytower is no more than twenty miles away. He'll need land and water for those beef, and the only way to get it is to take it. There's going to be a battle, and I knew your brother would want to help."

"What about the other farmers and ranchers?"

"I ain't had much time. I swung by the Queen ranch, on the way here, but no one was about. Don't know where Miller and his boys are."

"Big George and Von Gustin?"

"Haven't made it there yet." Bunion shrugged. "Don't even know a safe route up there anymore. Mallory got dragged behind a horse for crossing Black Diamond range. Unless a man is willing to ride five miles around, he can't even get to those places no more."

"I'll find Token and my brothers," Timony vowed. "Any help coming from town?"

"Not at the moment."

"See if you can get to Big George. I'm sure that he'll send Cully Deeks and a couple more to help."

"All right. Tell your brother to be careful. He's likely to find more bullets in the air than flies around a pigsty."

Timony shouted a good-bye as she was hurrying across the yard to get a horse saddled. Mallory had not deserted her. More than that, he had taken their side in a fight that was not his own. If that wasn't a sign that he still loved her, she didn't know what it could be.

The horse shied away at her hasty approach. Then, when she shouted at her, the mare trotted to the opposite

side of the corral. Panic drove Timony to chase the
horse, instead of coaxing her. In all, it took five minutes
to get a bridle on the mare. The seconds ticked by like
a speeding locomotive. The urge to move faster turned
her ten fingers to thumbs. Compounded with her racing
heart and the anxiety ripping at her chest, she was
clumsy and awkward at trying to secure the cinch. Once
atop the animal, however, she kicked the horse into a
run and raced out of the yard. Every second was critical.
She had to reach John and tell him what had happened.
Even as the wind blew into her face from the speed of
her mount, she feared their efforts would be too late.

*Darn your hide, Luke Mallory!* she steamed. *If you get
yourself killed before we have a chance to make up, I'll
never forgive you!*

Yarrow came in behind the three riders. He saw their
horses first, and veered off of the main trail until he
located them. It took a moment to realize what they had
in mind.

*Got to be Queen and his dimwit sons,* he decided. The
three of them were on foot, working their way up a draw
beyond the line shack. The Hereford bulls were in the
pasture, either lazing about or munching on grass. Easy
targets for three rifles.

Quanto was chopping wood near the front of the
house. Usually alert, he had not yet sensed any danger.
Yarrow thought of firing a shot to get his attention, but
then thought better of it. He reached into his saddlebag
and dug out his shaving mirror. By holding it to the
sunlight, he flashed it at the cabin.

Quanto caught sight of the reflection almost at once.
True to his warrior instincts, he did not react as if aware

of anything. Once Yarrow saw him put down the axe, he knew he'd gotten the signal. Quanto picked up an armload of wood and walked to the shack. He would have his rifle handy and be watching.

Yarrow skirted the hill, picking a trail that would bring him in above the Queens. He angled up to the crest, where he could put them under his gun, dismounted and pulled his rifle. Keeping low, so as not to be silhouetted against the sky, he eased over the top of the ridge and began working his way closer. He was two hundred yards away when he spied Quanto moving along the opposite side of the glen.

The three would-be executioners for the Hereford bulls were spreading out below. They were trying to take up positions where they could get the small herd in a crossfire. Yarrow had to shake his head at the stupidity of the idea. Three men with rifles, even good shots, were not likely to kill more than five or six bulls. A buffalo was dense enough that it would stand and wonder what the noise of gunfire meant, but not the cattle. After the first shot was fired, those animals would bolt and run.

Yarrow waited for Quanto to get within range. It was time to earn their money.

Miller was waving Dory to a better position, when the first shot came. Suddenly, Dory was no longer in sight. Chad was quick to react. He whirled toward the echo of the rifle fire and began to pump lead in that direction.

Miller dove for cover as a bullet sang off a rock right near his ear. He rolled onto his side and looked in that direction for a target. A second shot showed smoke. He ducked, but it would have been too late, had the shooter been aiming at him. The gunfire from Chad ceased and

Miller squirmed forward on his belly, burying himself in a small hollow between two clumps of sage.

"Dory?" he whispered. "Where you at, son?"

No answer.

"Chad?" he tried again. "Sound off!"

Only quiet.

Miller was immediately immersed in dread and sorrow. His boys were both down, maybe dying. He had been a fool to try and take out the herd of Herefords by himself. He should have listened to John and the others.

"You've no chance!" Yarrow called down to him. "You're done, Queen. If you want a fair shot, I'll give you one."

Miller lifted his head enough to see that Yarrow was coming down the incline, moving his way. He had a rifle in his hands. Another man was closing from the opposite direction. There was no escape.

Grief-stricken over the loss of his boys, Miller only wanted revenge. He didn't say a word, but jumped up to his feet, raising his rifle. He would take these two murdering scum with him. He would blast holes in them, spill their guts—

The bullet struck him between the shoulders. He didn't realize he'd been hit, until his face crashed against the earth and he suddenly had a mouthful of dirt. As blackness swooped in to cover his consciousness, he swore at his own asinine plan.

Cassie heard the distant shots. She wasn't aware of what was going on, but it was the first real chance she'd had to make her escape. With no thought of anything but getting away, she bolted from the cabin and ran as hard as she could.

The heavy skirt was not a good choice for sprinting, especially over bunch grass and sprawling sagebrush. She had gone less than a hundred yards when she was tripped up by her clothes getting tangled with a stand of brush. She sprawled headlong onto the ground, landing mostly on her elbows and knees. Gasping for breath, she scrambled up to her feet. It was then she spied the three horses, picketed in a gully. Lifting her skirt, she altered her route, racing toward the saddled mounts. No longer lost to desperation, she now had a means of escape.

The shooting had stopped, so it was a real concern that Quanto or Yarrow could return at any moment and discover she was missing. Panic hastened her footsteps, but she was keen enough to slow down for her approach of the horses. She had ridden only twice in her life, but she had no fear of getting on a horse. Her fear was of Yarrow, of what he would do once he knew she had gotten away!

Cassie sought the saddle with the shortest stirrup length, but they were all too long. She picked the most durable-looking horse and untied it. The animal turned to look at her, as if curious as to who she was, but it was well-trained enough that it allowed her to climb aboard. As her feet didn't reach the stirrups, she wedged them between the hobble straps. It would cause the vertical leather fenders to rub against the inside of her legs, but it was the only way to keep from bouncing around like a marble on a washboard.

Awkwardly, she used a double rein to turn the horse. Then, holding the guiding straps in either hand, she nudged the horse's ribs with her heels. Even as the animal broke into a trot, she was jostled up and down, completely out of time with the horse.

Cassie put one hand on the pommel and raised up slightly. It helped to a degree, but a sharp turn would have been enough to unseat her. Kicking her heels against the animal again, she urged more speed from the mount and hoped the horse was patient with the green rider on its back.

## Chapter Fourteen

Luke knelt between the two boulders and used his field glasses to watch the wagon and riders draw closer. Tito ducked low and came over to hunker down at his side.

"It them?" he asked.

"Yeah, they didn't waste any time."

"This isn't the way it was supposed to work, Mallory. I specifically remember you telling me we wouldn't be alone in this fight."

"Bunion was to spread the word. I didn't expect Hytower to move so quickly. He must have already gotten the news about us taking over the Irish claims."

"Makes sense to act before we get organized," Tito conjectured. "The longer the wait, the more chance we would get a plan worked out to stop them."

"Looks like two men on the wagon and three outriders. The lead man is a good hundred yards out in front. Appears as if the two side men have fanned out about as far too."

"Won't be able to surprise them as a group."

"I've never tucked the rifle butt against my cheek and started shooting at men who weren't trying to shoot back."

"This is your idea, Mallory. You want to give them the chance to tuck tails and run, I'll go along with it."

"You think that's smart?"

"About as smart as scratching your backside with a handful of yucca to cure an itch. It's sure to leave a host of cactus thorns in your hide."

"Then we open up on them from here?"

"Not a good idea either. They would circle and put us in a crossfire in no time."

"Tito, you aren't giving me a lot of options. We've got to stop that wagon. You're the one with all the war experience. If you remember, I've always been in the position of the man on the wagon, not the one trying to rob or stop it."

"Stop it," Tito replied, as if speaking to himself, "that might be the right approach."

Luke waited, able to see the man turning over a plan in his head. After a moment, Tito pointed down at the trail.

"See that ditch crossing?" At Luke's nod he said, "We can take the wagon."

"What about the outriders?"

"We let the lead man go right past. The other two will be too far out to do anything."

"All right, I'm with you until we grab the wagon. Then what?"

"Unhitch the horses and leave it sitting. No explosives—no problem. They fail."

Luke gave him an are-you-crazy stare. "You think once we detach the wagon, they are simply going to ride away?"

"Two of those guys look like cowpokes. Dawg is a tough nut with his fists, but I doubt if he could hit a bull from ten paces with a gun. I don't know about the guard on the wagon, but Chico is driving. He isn't going to buck us head-on.''

"If I'm not mistaken, they are still five against only the two of us.''

Tito grinned. "Watch it, Mallory. You're going to start scratching in the dirt and crowing at sunup.''

"Oh, now I'm a chicken! I thought I was being careful.''

"What's to be careful for? Your girl hates your guts. You haven't any reason to live.''

"Thanks for reminding me.''

"You got a better plan for stopping the wagon?''

"If I wasn't so against it, I'd say just shoot the horses.'' Luke grunted. "Guess we'll do it your way.''

"I don't want you blaming me, if I get us both killed. After all, it was your idea to get us into this war in the first place.''

"I only asked you to help. You didn't have to say yes.''

"Let's get a move on. They can't see the hollow from where they are, but every second we wait allows them to get that much closer.''

Luke followed Tito down the slight incline. At the base of the gully, each went off the main trail a few feet to either side. By pulling a small amount of brush and grass, they were able to make themselves a hiding place. Luke waited until Tito was totally concealed from view, then he lay down and pulled a tumbleweed and some dried grass over himself. Prone on his stomach, gun in hand, eyes half-lidded to keep out particles of dirt, Luke waited. His palm began to sweat, as he gripped the pistol tightly. He suffered the taste of dust in his mouth and nostrils, while his heart began to hammer louder and harder with each passing second.

*Luke, old boy,* he told himself, *this has got to be the most foolhardy thing you've ever done in your life. If Timony doesn't forgive you after this, she truly does hate you.*

The first horse approached after a time, the rider obviously cautious. These men knew that an ambush might be waiting. The lead man was ducked low in the saddle, offering a small target. His eyes never ceased moving from place to place, searching for anything out of the ordinary. Luke silently thanked the wind, for the breeze was blowing away from where they had picketed their horses. By the time the outrider's horse could pick up any scent, the wagon would have reached their position.

The creaking noise from the wheels turning against greased-but-worn axles combined with the plodding of the team of horses. Luke glimpsed the second outrider, beyond Tito's position, but he was unable to see the one who passed behind where he was in waiting. He hoped the fellow was at least a hundred yards away, before he jumped up to rush the wagon. If he was lagging behind, Luke might be popping right up into his line of sight. He'd sure get the last laugh about Tito's plan, if he was shot before he even got to the wagon.

Closer now, the horses slowed down for the rough rut at the bottom of the gully. They went across carefully and the front wagon wheels dipped into the ditch—

Tito sprang up as if he had been catapulted. Luke scrambled out, his gun aimed at the driver, Chico.

''Hold it!'' he shouted. ''One twitch and you're deader than a fence post!''

The guard was on the other side. He spun to meet Tito, his rifle in his hands, pointing, ready to fire.

Tito's gun belched fire and smoke. The man was stood up by the force of the slug hitting him in the chest. Even as he was sinking down on the wagon seat, Chico lifted his hands.

"Yonder they come!" Tito called. "Take cover!"

Luke threw a hasty look over his shoulder, to locate the outrider closest to him. It was just enough time to lose track of Chico. By the time he spied the man on horseback, Chico launched himself into the air. His body slammed against Luke and sent the gun flying from his fist. The two of them went down in a mix of arms and legs.

Luke rolled to throw Chico off, but it wasn't necessary. The man's only interest was in making his escape. By the time Luke recovered his pistol, bullets were slapping into the ground all around him. He dove for the protection of the wagon, hoping the horses didn't spook. If they took off, he and Tito would be downright naked out in the middle of the trail with no cover.

Tito had reached the wagon. He pushed the guard off onto the ground and shoved the brake into place. As Luke crawled under the bed, Tito ducked down under the wagon seat.

"They can't shoot at us without risking setting off the explosives!" Tito yelled.

"And that's supposed to make me feel good?" Luke called back between returning fire and using the wheel to hide his position.

The three riders had moved into shooting distance, all behind shelter, all using rifles. Chico ran and dodged through the brush until he linked up with one of the others. That put four guns against them and they could not retreat.

Tito shouted. ''Get to the tongue and unhitch the team.

''They are shooting real bullets out here, Tito!'' Luke hollered. ''Once the horses are gone, how do we get out of this alive?''

Tito raised up enough to fire, then quickly ducked for cover. ''I didn't make any promises about getting out alive. I only told you how we could stop the wagon.''

''That's great! If I set loose the horses, they might decide they have nothing to lose by taking aim at the explosives. What if the wagon blows?''

''Gripe, gripe, gripe,'' Tito replied. ''At least we'll go out with a bang!''

Timony spied the rider cutting across the open ground. A few head of cattle were near enough to lift their heads and take notice, but they immediately went back to grazing. Even at a great distance, Timony could see the ungainly jouncing of an inexperienced rider. There was something else, the flap of a woman's dress and the long auburn hair flowing in the wind. She put her heels to her own horse and cut a path that would intercept the rider.

Cassie saw her coming. For a moment, it appeared that she would turn her mount. Then, as if she recognized Timony, she continued, urging more speed from her horse. The two of them slowed to a stop as they intersected. Cassie's mount was blowing hard. Timony took note of the brand on its hip and raised her brows in surprise.

''That horse belongs to one of the Queen boys. They're the only ones in the valley with a Colorado brand.''

"If it is, I doubt they will be needing it back. I'm pretty sure that Quanto and Yarrow caught some men trying to reach the Herefords. There was a lot of shooting. I left as quickly as I could, but those two men are as cold-blooded as any I ever saw."

"Where are you going?"

Cassie lowered her eyes. "I wanted to tell your brother what was happening," she hesitated, "after I asked for sanctuary."

"Sanctuary?"

"I tried to warn your brother about Preston's plan at the Sunday Meeting last week. Yarrow was spying on me and told Preston."

"The divorce," Timony deduced. "I just heard about it from Bunion. He said it was final."

"The power of money," Cassie said.

"Then you're a free woman."

"Not while Yarrow is alive. Preston gave me to him."

Timony bridled. "What do you mean, he *gave* you to him? You're not a horse or pet to be given away!"

"I believe there is a gun law in Broken Spoke that is stronger than any law of right and wrong."

"Are they after you?"

"If not, they soon will be. I'm quite certain that Yarrow has an obsession about me. He has been making advances to me ever since Preston hired him. I hate him."

"Come with me. I know a place you can stay until this all blows over."

"What about your man?"

Timony looked at her. "My man?"

"He is in real danger. I overheard Yarrow and Quanto talking last night. For some reason, Yarrow came to talk to Quanto, before he told Preston about what had happened. I think the two of them have some kind of plan.''

''What are you talking about? What happened?''

''Mr. Mallory and his friends assumed the claims of the Irishmen. They have taken over the land which borders the creek.''

''Bunion told me. I was looking for Token and my brothers.''

''Yarrow said they would still probably try and alter the course of the creek. He had four or five of his men ready to take the explosives to the gap and blow it up. Once the creek has been turned, it will be twice as hard to get back to its old course.''

''When was that to take place?''

''Sounded like today.''

Timony was assailed by mixed emotions. Luke was back! He was risking his life to help her and the farmers. But he was in danger too. Yarrow's men were headed his way, intent upon changing the course of the Dakota Creek.

''Bunion stopped by to get my brothers to help. I thought they were with the cattle, but they must have gone down to see Dexter Cline and the farmers.''

''While they are busy talking, Yarrow's men will be blowing up the gap.''

Timony looked over Cassie's mount. The horse was nearly spent. ''The ranch house is over the next ridge. There is a woman there, her name is Linda. Tell her that I sent you. Have her hide you until I can find John. I must get help for Mr. Mallory.''

''I understand.''

Timony offered a smile of encouragement to the woman. ''It'll be okay.''

Cassie was too frightened to smile, but she did manage a nod of her head. "Linda?"

"That's her name."

"Thank you, Miss Fairbourn."

"Timony."

Cassie took a hasty look over her shoulder, but there were no riders closing in as yet. She turned back around. "Thank you, Timony."

"That way," Timony pointed a second time, "about a mile over the hill. I'll be back as soon as I can."

Cassie started her horse in that direction, while Timony pointed her little mare for Dexter Cline's farm. She hoped she wasn't too late to catch her brothers.

The rider came into their midst at a hard run. John held up his hand to stop their small procession. "Cully Deeks," he said, recognizing the foreman for Big George.

Cully pulled up hard, his horse skidding to a halt. He was out of breath. "They went yonder, not twenty minutes back! I was on my way to get some help."

"Who is yonder?"

"I've been keeping an eye on the Black Diamond. They sent five men out with a wagon load of explosives this morning. I had to keep watch until they reached the fork to town. They turned to the west, so I followed long enough to make sure they were headed for the gap."

"They're going to blow the gorge!" Billy deduced.

"We've got to stop them!" Token shouted. "Once they turn the creek, the whole valley will dry up and blow away."

"They've been stopped," Cully told them. "I heard

a lot of shooting over near the mouth of the canyon. Sounded like a real war going on.''

''Mallory!''

''I'd say.''

''Then their plan is going to fail. We've got them!''

''Not unless we give Mallory some help.''

Dexter Cline moved up. His boy was atop their only horse. ''Sounds like we're heading for trouble, John. I'd as soon my boy wasn't along.''

''You can head back to your place. We can handle it.''

But Dexter shook his head. ''I'm going.'' As the boy slid off the back of the horse, he turned to speak to him. ''Get on home, son. Tell your ma I'll be fine.''

''Yeah, Pa, I'll tell her.''

''Let's ride!'' John called out, digging in his heels. He led the other four men, Billy, Token, Dexter and Cully, urging his horse into a hard run.

Billy had the fastest horse. He was alongside within a hundred yards. ''Sure hope we're not too late.''

''If anything happens to Mallory, Timony will hang all of us out to dry like so much laundry.''

Billy leaned forward and pulled ahead. ''Come on, big brother. I'd rather be skinned alive than have her after my hide!''

## Chapter Fifteen

Quanto stopped his horse and examined the ground. "She met up with another rider," he informed Yarrow. "Looks as if one of them went to the ranch and the other went toward Cline's farm."

Yarrow looked both directions. "Why would she go to Cline's place?"

"And where is the other horse going? To get help?"

"Which one do you think is her horse?"

"Can't tell on this hillside. Been too many cattle milling about. If not for the dew this morning, we wouldn't be able to follow tracks at all."

"Whoever she met up with must have told her to go to Cline's place."

"Makes sense," Quanto agreed. "We would expect her to head for Fairbourn's ranch. The other rider probably figured to send her off to a place we wouldn't think to look."

"Let's go."

They moved with a purpose, their horses' gait an easy lope. Yarrow was anxious, but in no hurry. Cassie could not have gone far. By virtue of their guns, no one would stand against the two of them. Once he had that woman again, he would see to it she never pulled a stunt like this a second time. He would chain her to the wall if necessary. Marriage or not, she was going to belong to him body and soul.

"Hey! Look over there!" Quanto said, pointing toward someone on foot.

Yarrow neck-reined in that direction. They easily overtook the young Cline boy and stopped right in his path. His eyes grew wide with fright, at their arrival, but he stood his ground.

"What are you doing out here, sonny?" Quanto asked him.

"I'm on my way home."

"How'd you get way out here? You chasing squirrels or something?"

"I know who you are," the boy said, diverting his attention from Quanto to Yarrow. "You're the gunman, Yarrow."

"You see another rider pass by here in the past few minutes?"

"From a distance," he admitted. "Looked like Timony Fairbourn, but I ain't for certain. She didn't see me."

Quanto frowned at the news. "Appears we guessed wrong."

"Maybe, or the boy here might have been too far away to recognize which girl it was."

"Won't make any difference," Quanto continued. "We'll get her back."

"Where's your pa, sonny?" Yarrow asked. "He at the house?"

"He and the Fairbourn crew are on their way to wipe out your men, Yarrow. If I was you, I'd light a'shuck out of the country."

"Wipe out my men? What're you talking about?"

"You sent your wagon of explosives to the gap, but it didn't make it. Luke Mallory has done stopped it. My pa and the others are on their way to make sure it don't go no further. I'd say Mr. Hytower has about run his rope in Broken Spoke. Come August and September, without the water from Dakota Creek, his big herd of cattle are going to be dropping in their tracks from thirst."

Yarrow and Quanto exchanged a nervous glance. Quanto asked: "How do you know so much?"

"Cully Deeks has been watching your place. He came to tell us."

Quanto rotated to glare at Yarrow. "See what keeping an eye on that stupid woman has done? I wasn't able to make any patrols!"

Yarrow lifted a hand to silence him. "You'd better get on home, kid."

Young Cline did not hesitate. He took off at a run.

"What now?" Quanto asked, as soon as the boy was out of earshot.

Yarrow sighed. "If the kid told us right and Mallory stopped the wagon, we might have to change to the second plan we talked about last night. Sounds as if Preston is going to lose his chance to get the creek rerouted. His five thousand head of cattle are going to be pushed out into the wasteland, too far to even water."

Quanto grunted cynically. "I've looked over the lay of the land, Yarrow. This was not a good choice for Hytower in the first place. Without taking over the entire valley, there isn't enough grazing and water to handle a herd the size he has coming."

The saddle creaked under Yarrow's weight, as he leaned around to look off in the direction of the gap.

They were too far away to hear any gunfire, but there was no reason to think the boy had not told them the truth. If the Fairbourn bunch and some of the others were in the fight, his hired men had little or no chance in a fight.

"Maybe we ought to draw our time, Quanto. I've taken a peek into the safe Preston keeps at the house. You think he'll open it for us?"

Quanto chuckled. "Could be, if we ask him real nice."

"I'd say this here job has gone sour. We ought to pick up the pay we have coming and maybe mosey out of this part of the country."

"What about your girl?"

"I'll make a stop on the way out of the valley. She's either at the Fairbourn place or over at Cline's farm. I don't think anyone is willing to die to keep her."

"You got it bad."

Yarrow did not deny it. "I wanted her from the minute I first saw her, Quanto. Now that I've got her away from Hytower, I'm going to keep her."

"Let's go collect our money."


"How you doing up there?" Luke called.

"Running low on ammo. You think anyone ever uses this road?"

"If you are expecting some helpful Samaritans to drop by, you can forget it."

"Those boys are fair shots. I've been nicked twice."

"Let's hope their aim stays true. Shooting into a load of explosives is not a good idea. You hit bad?"

"Only scratches. How about you?"

"I was smart enough to get under the wagon. You're the one they can see to get a good shot at."

"Yeah, I was thinking the same thing," Tito said. "You figure that, once we run out of bullets, they might let us leave?"

"Ask the one you shot."

Tito reared up and fired, then ducked back for cover. "I'm beginning to think maybe this wasn't a good idea."

Luke was searching for an escape route. They could release the team of horses and make a run for cover. Without being able to move the wagon, the fight would be ended. But how to do it, without getting shot full of holes? Plus, once the men from Black Diamond saw what they were up to, they would know they had lost the chance to blow the gap. There would be no reason not to try and kill Tito and him by any means necessary.

Suddenly, there came several gunshots. Luke thought the four men were mounting an assault, until he saw them scrambling for their horses.

"Hey! It's the calvary!" Tito shouted.

"Get out!" Luke shouted. "Run for it!"

Tito realized the danger at the same instant. He jumped to the ground, as Luke scrambled out from under the wagon. If Dawg's first shot had set off the explosives, it would have blown them both to bits. As it was, he had to fire three times.

Tito had trouble finding his feet. Luke grabbed him under the arm and they began to race for safety.

A deafening blast went off in their ears. It was as if God had swatted them both with a great fly swatter. They were lifted off of the ground, thrown thirty feet, then slammed into the earth, while pieces of wood and debris pelted them like a deadly hail.

Luke awoke to discover himself facedown on the ground. It felt as if the biggest buffalo in the herd had used his body for a ground blanket. He blinked against the swirl of dust and smoke, turning his head enough to find Tito at his side.

"Tito? You dead?" he whispered hoarsely.

The man lay motionless for a full minute, before he began to stir. "Get the name of the driver on that stage," he muttered. "I'll teach him to run over me."

A personal survey revealed their clothes were singed and even shredded in a place or two from the blast. Bits of rock and splinters of wood had been imbedded in their back and legs from the explosion. Miraculously, there were no broken bones.

"You boys don't look no worse for wear," Dexter Cline announced, as he approached the two of them. "I expected to find you in several pieces each."

"You mean I'm in one piece?" Luke asked, working his aching body to a sitting position.

"Look about the same as one of the steaks my Helen tenderizes before cooking it," he replied. "She uses a rough-edge hammer I made her." He laughed. "Couldn't have done a better job than that there exploding wagon."

"That was something," Billy added, having arrived too. "Thought you two were goners for sure."

"What about Hytower's men?"

"Cully, Token and John have them pinned down," Billy answered. "They can't hold out for long."

"As you two are back in the mix, we'll get them quick enough," Dexter put in. "If you're through loafing, it's time to finish this fight!"

\* \* \*

Preston scowled at the two men. "What's the idea, Yarrow? You can't up and quit!"

"We did our share, Hytower," Yarrow replied. "We saved the lives of your precious Hereford bulls, but it won't change the tally. This here dispute is lost."

"What about my Herefords?"

"We killed the Queen boys. That ought to be worth something."

He was still confused. "You killed all three of them?"

"This here was a high-stakes game, Hytower. We ain't been playing for pine nuts."

Quanto slung an empty saddlebag over his shoulder and rested his hand on the butt of his pistol. "Just pay us what you owe us, Preston. We aren't going to stick around here until the locals drag us before a local judge and jury. We'd end up swinging from the end of a rope."

"That's ridiculous!" Preston sputtered. "I control the governor of the territory! I can get our own judge appointed to preside over any hearing. If those men were on my land, attempting to kill my prize bulls, no one is going to condemn your actions."

Yarrow grunted. "Hate to be the one to toss a dead rat into your stewpot, Preston, but we've made up our minds. You'll need to hire more men with less brains if you're going to try and pull off this land and water deal."

"There's no need to panic. We can still win this battle. Stick with me for a little longer."

Quanto shook his head. "You lost your claim on the land you needed, and we heard the wagon of explosives has been stopped by now. You might not be the big stick you think. We ain't going to take the chance of being arrested and hauled off to jail, no matter what you say."

Preston put a sorrowful look on Yarrow. "I'm very disappointed in both of you. I never would have taken you men for quitters."

"I'll risk my life with a gun in my hand, but I'm not going to put my life in the hands of a jury, even if you do have some pull with the judge."

"All right, if you want to turn tail and run!" Preston stormed over to the safe. He spun the dials and worked the lock. "I'll give you the rest of the month and a couple hundred each for expenses. That ought to be fair."

He pulled open the door and the blast of a gun rocked the room. Preston slumped to the floor without a sound. Yarrow blinked from the noise, then put a mock surprise on his face. "Ye-cats! Quanto. I told you to be careful with that hair-trigger Colt. You've done shot the boss."

"You suppose he'll be upset about it?"

"Probably fire us on the spot."

"I really hate the thought of being fired. Let's just throw our tack on a horse and get out of here."

"Sounds like a good plan, Quanto, but we'd better take the money out of the safe. Wouldn't want some sneaky thief coming in here and stealing it."

"You're right. There are some real unsavory sorts around here. I wouldn't trust none of them with that kind of money."

Yarrow moved over and used the toe of his boot to shove Preston's body out of the way. He then knelt down and began to pull out the stack of money.

Quanto forked over the saddlebag and watched with interest, as Yarrow began sticking in money by the handful. "Real careless of Hytower to keep so much cash in the house. It's a wonder he wasn't robbed."

"Lucky for him we're here to see that nobody steals it."

"What about the girl?" Quanto wanted to know. "You still think she's worth the effort?"

"I've got a mind to have her," he admitted. "But you don't have to help. We'll split the money here and now."

"Good thing the divorce went through or the poor kid would be a widow."

Yarrow paused and checked the count on the money. "Looks like a couple thousand each. Gives us a pretty good bonus. The job worked out after all." He shook his head. "Too bad there isn't anything left for the others."

"If that Cline kid told us straight, those guys won't be coming back anyhow."

"Let's get our tack and war bags. Time we left Broken Spoke in our dust."

Dawg's eyes were wide with shock as he breathed his last breath. He had been the last one to try and shoot it out with John's party. Token said he thought the bullet came from his gun, but it could have been either him or John or Billy. Only Dexter had not been shooting in the man's direction.

"You men have a choice," John was telling the three survivors, "either take your horses and get out of the country, or take your chances in front of a judge."

The three exchanged glances, but it was Chico who raised his hand as a sign of surrender. "Without Hytower owning the property, we're beat. You mind if I swing by the ranch and get my gear?"

"You've got a horse and your life," Token growled. "That's all you get."

The three men didn't argue further. As a group, they gathered up the horses and rode off in the direction of Rimrock.

As they disappeared down the trail, a rider came from the opposite direction. John held up a hand to block the glare of the sun.

"Looks like Timony."

"What's she coming out here for?" Dexter asked.

Billy nudged him with an elbow. "Maybe she was worried about someone."

"Oh," Dexter replied, looking in the direction of the still-smoking wagon.

Timony rode hard, not pulling up until she was within a few feet. With the move of a practiced rider, she was off before the horse skidded to a jarring halt.

"Fight's over, Sis," Billy said.

Timony looked at the dead man on the ground. Her eyes quickly found a second body down by the smoldering wagon.

"Where is Luke?"

John was hesitant to answer, while Billy looked at Dexter and both Cully and Token had eyes only for the toes of their boots.

"Well?" she asked, immediately fearful.

"He'll be okay," John finally assured her. "He was . . . injured when the wagon exploded."

"Luke's hurt?"

"Now, Timmy . . ."

"Where is he?"

Billy was the one who stepped up. He pointed to show the way. "Down there, in the ditch, behind that stand of brush. Tito is trying to patch him up." As she hurried down the hill, he called, "Don't worry, Sis, I think he'll be okay."

Timony scrambled down the hill at a run, but Luke suddenly appeared! He popped up from behind the brush so quickly that she nearly fell down trying to put on her brakes. Oddly, Luke had a red tint to his face. She was about to ask about his condition, when Tito rose up next to him. There was a sheepish look about his expression.

"They said you were hurt," she said, staring at one and then at the other.

"Wagon splinters," Tito explained. "Luke removed a couple from my shoulder and I removed a couple from his . . . back."

She frowned at the way he said the last word—back! About the time she opened her mouth to question them further, she noticed that Luke was hitching his belt. "Oh . . ." she murmured, "I didn't know. . . ."

"He'll be fine," Tito showed a toothy grin, "once he can sit down again."

"Thanks, Tito," Luke snapped the words. "I knew I could count on your discretion."

Timony ducked her head, but she was unable to hide the smile. Tito began to chuckle, then laughed out loud. She couldn't help herself. She began to laugh too.

Luke finally gave a good-natured smile at them both. "I've always wondered what it would be like to end up the *butt* of someone's joke."

The sound of steps turned him around. John was approaching on foot. Before he could speak, Timony crossed over to meet him. She whispered to him in hushed tones. John listened intently, then whirled around and took off on a run, heading back for his horse.

"What's up?" Luke asked, moving up to her side.

"There's a lady visitor at our ranch. She is asking for protection from Yarrow."

"We'd best tag along," Tito suggested. "John's a good man, but Yarrow is quick as they come with a pistol. Hate to see John get in over his head."

"Think your brother will lend me a horse?"

"Can you ride?"

He might have laughed, but she was deadly serious. "It was only a splinter. I could have handled it alone, but the back of your lap is a tough place to reach."

Timony started to take a step, but Luke caught hold of her and pulled her to him. "Before you go, I've been wanting to tell you something."

She gave him a direct look. "Like the fact that you took out a claim on this land, so that you could protect our water rights?"

"No."

"Or maybe that you were going to risk your life to help us?"

"Not that either."

"So what did you want to tell me?"

He didn't say anything, but he took her firmly in his arms and kissed her. She did not squirm or fight. In fact, she was so receptive that Billy whistled and called: "Get him, Sis!"

"I thought she'd dropped Mallory from her dance card," Token observed.

"Guess he's a good dancer," Billy joked.

Timony finally broke contact. She was gasping for air and pushed away from Luke.

"How about letting a girl catch her breath?"

"There isn't much of a house on this place, but there's

plenty of water. I figure we can get us a few head of cattle, a flock of chickens, maybe even a couple of pigs. We'll do just fine.''

"What do you mean, we?"

"You going to tell me that kiss didn't mean anything?"

She waved her hand. "It was only a thank-you kiss! It didn't mean anything.''

"Yeah, well, if you ever kiss another man like that, I'll bury him under six feet of dirt.''

"Oh, you can threaten some nonexistent person, but you can't even ask me to marry you properly?''

Luke looked at the distant form of John Fairbourn. "I don't have time at the moment. John might need some help.''

He took a step, but Timony caught hold of his arm. "John can take care of himself, mister,'' her words were hedged with ice. "I'm not going to pine over you for another six months.''

Tito was already on a horse, following after John. "Timony, I . . .'' he looked up the hill. Billy was grinning from ear to ear and both Token and Cline were watching. "This isn't the right time or place.''

"I let you kiss me in front of them,'' she reminded him. "What kind of girl does that make me look like?''

The fires of embarrassment heated his face, but he swallowed the chagrin and looked into Timony's eyes. "I think you're the most beautiful woman in the world,'' he said softly.

"Oh?"

"Yeah,'' he mumbled. "I reckon I would lay down my life for the chance to hold you in my arms again.''

"And?" she prodded, as he sought the words that would satisfy her.

"And I reckon I love you."

"Not good enough," she said. "Do you want me for your wife?"

"Of course."

"Then ask me!"

He swallowed a hard lump. "Will you marry me?"

She backed up a step. "No."

He was dumbfounded. "No?"

Then she laughed. "Not until you build me a decent house. I'm not going to live in one of those shacks the Irish threw together."

"Then the answer is yes?"

"What are you standing here for?" she replied. "John might be in trouble. You'd better take care of him. He'll be your brother-in-law one day soon."

"Yeah," Luke groaned, "Why didn't I think of offering to help?"

Billy rode down the hill, stepped to the ground, and turned over his horse to Luke. "I'll round up your horses and catch the team from the wagon. We'll be along."

Luke swung aboard and started off. He was consumed by a lightness in his chest that made him forget about the tender spot that occasionally bounced against the saddle. Timony had not only forgiven him, she was going to marry him! All he had to do was finish off the job against the Black Diamond. Small concession for the prize of a lifetime.

Cassie could not remain in the next room. When Yarrow knocked Linda down, she hurried out of her hiding place.

"Stop it!" she cried. "You don't have to hurt her!"

Yarrow shook his head in mock wonderment. "How can you keep playing me like a fish on the line, Cassie? Anyone would think you don't want me."

"Anyone but you," she scathed. "You're too ignorant to understand the word no!"

"I understand it all right," he showed a satisfied smirk, "I just don't accept it."

"I hate your every fiber, Yarrow! You disgust me! I will die before I ever submit to you!"

He chuckled. "I see you haven't quite made up your mind about me. But that's okay. I'll give you some time—say a couple years."

"I'm not going with you."

"Darn, gal!" Yarrow drew his gun and pointed it at Linda. "I don't think this woman can live with a decision like that."

"You wouldn't kill her!" Cassie was incredulous. "Not even you would kill a woman!"

"Wearing a dress don't make all that much difference to me, sweetheart. Why don't you come along like a nice girl and there won't be any trouble."

John appeared behind him. At the relief and immediate warmth in Cassie's face, Yarrow whirled about—

With a solid downward chop, John knocked the gun from Yarrow's hand. The gunman backed away, both hands lifted in surrender.

"Hold on there, Fairbourn," he blurted quickly, fearfully. "There's no need to get physical. I was only politely asking the lady to come with me."

"He about knocked my teeth loose!" Linda shouted. "Hit me right in the face!"

John doubled his fists. ''I told you that I'd catch you without your gun one day.''

Yarrow retreated until his back was against the wall. ''Hey! No contest, old buddy. I concede, you're a better man with your fists than I am.''

But John was not satisfied. He hammered Yarrow several solid shots, with a vengeance.

Tito came through the door as John sent Yarrow sprawling onto his face. They stood back, watching the gunman. Without a gun in his fist, he was like a snake without fangs. He lay there, too cowardly to get up, counting on John being the kind of man who would not hit him while he was lying on the floor.

John stood over him, ''Get up and take your medicine, you miserable excuse for a man!''

Tito was not looking when Quanto entered behind him. The gun in his ribs was enough to convince him that the tables had been turned.

''Back off of him, Fairbourn,'' Quanto snarled. ''Yarrow! Let's get out of here!''

Yarrow spat out a bit of blood and picked up his gun. John had split his lip and crushed his nose flat. He holstered the weapon, then took a swipe at a trickle of blood.

''You got a punch like the kick of a mule, Fairbourn,'' he said. ''Now we've done it your way, how about we do it mine?'' He eased his gun in and out of his holster, prepared to draw.

''No!'' Cassie cried. She rushed between the two men. ''You don't have to kill him, Yarrow. I'll go with you.''

John tensed, lowering his hand to just above his gun. He knew he had no chance against Yarrow's speed.

Quanto shrugged, "Draw when you want, Fairbourn," he said, keeping his attention on Tito. "But let's keep it a fair fight."

"Fair would be if you wanted to take me on, Yarrow," Tito replied.

"If you kill him, you'll never have me!" Cassie continued in her effort to save John's life. "I swear it, Yarrow. You hurt him and I'll never submit to you. I'll die first!"

"You sure that female is worth all this effort?" Quanto asked.

"If something is worth having, it's worth fighting for," Yarrow replied, pushing her roughly to one side. Then his cold, deadly eyes rested on John. "Whenever you want to draw your last breath, Fairbourn. I'll give you first go at your gun. Can't ask for anything more fair than that."

John's heart hammered in his chest. He was shaking inside, but forced his body to obey his commands. With a deliberate effort, he backed up a step and spread his feet into a fighting stance.

"Drop the gun!" Luke said, moving in behind Quanto.

"For the love of—" Yarrow swore. "Why didn't you shut the door behind you, Quanto?"

Quanto hesitated, thinking hard, then he pitched his gun to one side—right out the window! When it shattered the glass, he spun and charged into Luke. The two of them were propelled out the door.

Luke heard a scream from inside the house, followed by two quick shots. However, he was busy with Quanto. They crashed to the porch and rolled into the yard. Luke was not fully recovered from his numerous injuries, but he still got in a good punch to the man's jaw. Quanto used his left hand to keep Luke's gun pointed away from his body, but it allowed Luke to land another solid left to the side of his head.

Instead of trying to fight back, Quanto used his free hand to shake Luke off of him, and slapped at the gun to knock it loose. It might have worked, except for Tito stepping outside. When he stuck the muzzle of his pistol up to the back of the man's head, Quanto instantly ceased his struggle.

"I heard shooting!" Luke said, getting up onto his feet and dusting himself off.

"Yarrow wasn't as fast as he thought. The second shot was his—sure enough killed an innocent board in the wall."

"John?"

"He and the lady are inside, I'd guess discussing her future."

Linda appeared on the porch. She was still fingering the welt on her chin. "I think you'll find that these two snakes have done something to Mr. Hytower. When they arrived, they talked as if he was not going to be around anymore."

"Anything you want to say, Quanto?"

"Yarrow killed Hytower."

"You believe him, Mallory?" Tito asked.

"If he was shot with a .32 caliber gun," Luke answered back. "Quanto here carries a .45."

Tito found a piece of rope and tied Quanto's hands behind his back. They hauled Yarrow out of the house, a few minutes ahead of the arrival of Billy, Token, Cully, Dexter, and Timony."

Before the details of the fight could be outlined, Bunion rode into the yard.

"Looks like everything came to a head," he said, taking notice of Yarrow draped over his horse and the bound Quanto.

"They sent the wagon of explosives to blow up the gap," Billy told him. "Those fellers are either dead or on their way out of the country."

"I was trying to circle around the Black Diamond spread and found the three Queen men, all dead."

Quanto said: "They were there to kill the Hereford bulls."

"I decided to see what Hytower knew about it," Bunion went on. "When I stopped at his house, I found him dead. The safe was open and had been cleaned out."

"We found the money in the saddlebags. Quanto claims Yarrow killed him."

Bunion reached into his vest pocket. "The bullet went right through his brisket and was lodged in the wall. Looks to be a .44 or .45." He squinted at Quanto. "I recollect seeing Yarrow usually packed himself a .32."

Luke glanced over at Quanto. The man lowered his head in defeat. It was pretty obvious he knew his lie would not hold up in front of a judge. A rope or a long prison sentence awaited the remainder of Quanto's life.

Tito mounted his horse and took the lead rope of Quanto's horse. Bunion took hold of the one Yarrow's body was tied to.

"We'll take these two into town."

"I'll ride over with Cully and pick up the bodies of Miller and his sons," Dexter offered.

"Guess I'll tag along," Token said.

"I might as well bring the wagon and come too,"

Billy offered. ''We can pick up Hytower, while we're at it.''

Within minutes, Linda had returned to the foreman's house. It left only Luke, Timony, John, and Cassie in the yard.

''What about you, ma'am?'' Luke asked Cassie. ''What will you do now?''

''Uncle Mont—that is my ex-uncle—will very likely inherit Preston's ranch. I'm sure he'll have room for me.''

''You've a big herd headed this way,'' Timony said.

''I think he'll want to ship most of that herd to the auction yards back east. He once told me that if the old Renikie place was his he would sell or lease out the Hereford bulls. Then he wouldn't have to watch over a great number of cattle.''

''We'd likely take him up on a deal like that,'' John said. ''Those bulls are the beef of the future.''

Timony eyed the girl curiously. ''So you are going to stay in Broken Spoke, Cassie?''

Cassie flicked a glance at John. ''Yes, I like it here.''

John appeared uncomfortable as both Luke and Timony were staring at him. He cleared his throat and asked: ''You two make peace?''

Timony slipped over next to Luke. His arm automatically went around her waist and he pulled her closer.

''We're working on it, Big Brother,'' she said, raising quickly up onto her toes to give Luke a quick peck on the lips. Luke would have snagged a little better kiss, but Timony was too smart to linger within his grasp. She ducked away and moved to a safe distance. ''Soon as old cold feet here gets me into a wedding gown.''

"And builds her a better house," Luke told him. "Reckon we'll make good neighbors?"

John smiled at the radiant glow in his sister's face. "Yeah," he said sincerely, "I think you'll both be just fine."